AN IMPOSSIBLE CRIME

"The last person to touch the dagger was Mr. Fane himself. Wasn't it?"

"It was," Sharpless said abruptly.

"He was sitting there," pursued Ann, puckering up her face, "with the revolver and the dagger in his hands. It was a rubber dagger then. Because I remember him twisting it back and forth. Then *you*—" Ann looked at Rich—"told him to put the revolver and the dagger on that little table. He got up, and went to the table, and put them down, and came back here. *But not one of the rest of us has been anywhere near that table since.*"

"You're quite a detective, Miss Browning," Rich observed, and the color rose in her face. "I can't help agreeing. It is true. And in that case . . ."

Ann frowned.

"Well, you see, in that case it means that somebody who wasn't in the room must have sneaked in to exchange the rubber dagger with the real dagger."

"But," Sharpless said rather wildly, "that's impossible. I've got eyes. I've got ears. I'll take my Bible oath, I'll swear to my dying day, that nobody came here either by the windows or by the door!"

And, as a matter of fact, he was perfectly right.

THE BESTSELLING NOVELS
BEHIND THE BLOCKBUSTER MOVIES—
ZEBRA'S MOVIE MYSTERY GREATS!

HIGH SIERRA (2059, $3.50)
by W.R. Burnett
A dangerous criminal on the lam is trapped in a terrifying web of circumstance. The tension-packed novel that inspired the 1955 film classic starring Humphrey Bogart and directed by John Houston.

MR. ARKADIN (2145, $3.50)
by Orson Welles
A playboy's search to uncover the secrets of financier Gregory Arkadin's hidden past exposes a worldwide intrigue of big money, corruption—and murder. Orson Welles's only novel, and the basis for the acclaimed film written by, directed by, and starring himself.

NOBODY LIVES FOREVER (2217, $3.50)
by W.R. Burnett
Jim Farrar's con game backfires when his beautiful victim lures him into a dangerous deception that could only end in death. A 1946 cinema classic starring John Garfield and Geraldine Fitzgerald. (AVAILABLE IN FEBRUARY 1988)

BUILD MY GALLOWS HIGH (2341, $3.50)
by Geoffrey Homes
When Red Bailey's former lover Mumsie McGonigle lured him from the Nevada hills back to the deadly hustle of New York City, the last thing the ex-detective expected was to be set up as a patsy and framed for a murder he didn't commit. The novel that inspired the screen gem OUT OF THE PAST, starring Robert Mitchum and Kirk Douglas. (AVAILABLE IN APRIL 1988)

Available wherever paperbacks are sold, or order direct from the Publisher. Send cover price plus 50¢ per copy for mailing and handling to Zebra Books, Dept. 2928, 475 Park Avenue South, New York, N.Y. 10016. Residents of New York, New Jersey and Pennsylvania must include sales tax. DO NOT SEND CASH.

CARTER DICKSON
SEEING IS BELIEVING

ZEBRA BOOKS
KENSINGTON PUBLISHING CORP.

ZEBRA BOOKS

are published by

Kensington Publishing Corp.
475 Park Avenue South
New York, NY 10016

Copyright © 1941 by William Morrow & Company, Inc.
Copyright renewed 1969 by John Dickson Carr.

All rights reserved. No part of this book may be reproduced in any form or by any means without the prior written consent of the Publisher, excepting brief quotes used in reviews.

First Zebra Books printing: March, 1990

Printed in the United States of America

One

One night in midsummer, at Cheltenham in Gloucestershire, Arthur Fane murdered a nineteen-year-old girl named Polly Allen.

That was the admitted fact.

The girl was only an incident in his life; but she had fallen for him, and was threatening to make trouble with his wife. She even mentioned marriage. In Cheltenham, everybody has to be respectable. Arthur Fane, as head of the firm of Fane, Fane & Randall, family solicitors, had to be particularly respectable.

So, one night when Vicky Fane, Uncle Hubert, and the two servants were away, he invited this girl to his house. She came there secretly, expecting a party, and was strangled with her own imitation-silk scarf. During the dark hours of the night Arthur Fane put her body into his car, drove up Leckhampton Hill, and buried her near the old quarry there.

Polly Allen was a girl of doubtful origins, who drifted from town to town, reasonably respectable but with no family or particular friends; it seemed unlikely that anybody would inquire after her. And, in fact, nobody ever did. Her murder remains unproved and in general even unsuspected to the present day.

But two persons found out about it—Hubert Fane,

Arthur's uncle, when it happened; and Vicky Fane, his wife, a little later.

To Vicky the realization came with slowly growing horror. She was a pretty, likeable, pleasant girl of twenty-five years as opposed to Arthur's thirty-eight. She had been married to him for two years, and was beginning quietly, strongly to dislike him even before this happened.

Realization came in patches. On the day following the murder, Vicky found Polly Allen's handkerchief, with Polly's name stitched in it, pushed down out of sight behind the cushion of an easy chair in the drawing room. She burned the handkerchief in case the servants should find it. After a time she made discreet inquiries, and discovered that Polly seemed to have left town. That meant only casual infidelity, of course. But then, during the hot nights with the moon shining on him, Arthur Fane began to talk in his sleep.

Vicky listened, white-faced in the dark. She had to *know*, and she guessed who else knew, by his altered position in the household since the night of July fifteenth.

Hubert Fane.

Uncle Hubert Fane had come to stay with them in April. "Just a brief visit, my boy, while I look round." He arrived back in England vaguely from "the colonies." He was supposed to have money, and was greeted by Arthur with expansive hospitality. But by the end of May he was still there, without giving any sign of getting a place for himself or even of standing his round of drinks when they dropped in at The Plough.

On the contrary, he began borrowing a pound or two, here and there: "until I can cash a check, dear boy." By June, Arthur was fed up. By July he was on the point of bluntly giving Uncle Hubert his walking papers, when the night of July fifteenth changed all that.

Uncle Hubert was then moved to a sunnier bedroom on the side of the house facing the front lawn. His borrowings became more frequent. If he expressed preferences to Arthur in the matter of a dish for dinner, Vicky was curtly told to get it.

Now this makes out Hubert Fane to be a common variety of blackmailer, which he was not. Vicky liked him; everybody liked him. Hubert Fane, fiftyish, was a lean, distinguished-looking man with gray-white hair. Vicky knew him for an old rogue; but a modest, unassuming, almost kind-hearted rogue. He always dressed well, in shadings of gray; he was widely traveled, well-read, and of irreproachable manners. Though he talked in somewhat elaborate, flowery sentences, he talked entertainingly and not without wit.

Even the retired army officers of Cheltenham liked him. These he treated with a sort of grave deference: as, say, a subaltern would treat his colonel. Without mentioning his rank or regiment, he contrived to suggest that he too was experienced in campaigns—not as much as they, of course; but still enough to listen to their stories with appreciation. "Not a bad chap," was the verdict; "not a bad chap at all."

So Uncle Hubert knew; and, under pressure from Vicky, admitted it, though not in such a way as could compromise him.

Vicky never forgot the afternoon when all this came out. It was a hot afternoon towards the end of August, when all the windows were set open and not a breath of air stirred. She sat with Hubert in the back drawing room (where Polly Allen had been strangled), looking out over a scarlet rose garden.

Uncle Hubert sat opposite her, smiling an agreeable smile under his large nose.

"But—*murder!*" Vicky whispered.

"Sh-h!" urged Uncle Hubert, not at all easy about this himself. "It was indiscreet," he conceded. "I cannot help feeling it was indiscreet. Still, there it is. These things happen."

Vicky looked at him helplessly.

Brown-haired, blue-eyed, with a sturdy body and a taste for outdoor exercise, she might have been any young upper-middle-class wife. She was a good wife: she managed Arthur's home efficiently, and had a way with servants. Everything seemed normal except this one black image.

Uncle Hubert cleared his throat.

"I am sure," he pursued, "that if you talk the matter over with Arthur, quietly—"

"Talk it over? I couldn't even go *near* him with a story like that!"

Uncle Hubert regarded her anxiously.

"Then I hope, my dear, that you are not meditating any such regrettable step as—er—going near the authorities? There is the family honor to consider."

"Family honor!" said Vicky. Her sick rage blinded her. "Family honor! All you're thinking about is your meal-ticket. You've been blackmailing Arthur and you know it."

Uncle Hubert looked genuinely shocked and hurt. His distress was, in fact, so evident that at any other time Vicky would have comforted him.

"Now there, my dear," he pointed out, "you wrong me. You really do wrong me. Candor compels me to admit that I may have mentioned the matter to the boy, and expressed my sympathy for him in his awkward predicament. That is all. No transaction of a sordid financial nature, I give you my word, has ever been so much as mentioned between us."

"No," said Vicky thoughtfully. "You wouldn't need to. Either of you."

"Thank you, my dear. If I seem to sense some latent irony in your tone, I trust I am well-bred enough to overlook it. Thank you."

"How did you learn about it?"

"I was curious. That Arthur should send you overnight to visit your mother was reasonable enough. That he should give the servants the night off was still plausible. But that he should provide me with a ticket to hear Gigli sing at the Colston Hall in Bristol and offer to pay both my railway fare and my hotel bill there, was simply incredible.

"Nor did I like his extra remark that he would be working very late at the office. Unsuspicious as I am by nature, I still felt that something must be up. So I did not go to Bristol. I returned here, feeling that in justice to you I ought to keep an eye on him."

"And you *saw*—?"

"Well . . ."

"Yet you didn't interfere?"

The old villain had at least the grace to look uncomfortable here. But his tone was persuasive.

"My dear, what could I do? I could not know what was in Arthur's mind. I anticipated something of a merely vulgar nature; and was looking forward to it, I must confess, with considerable interest. The unfortunate incident occurred before anybody could have interfered. It was on that sofa there, where you are sitting now. . . ."

Vicky leaped up from it, feeling as though someone had squeezed her heart.

"Afterwards I could hardly embarrass the boy by betraying my presence. There is such a thing as decency, my dear."

This wasn't real, Vicky told herself.

She folded her arms, cradling them as though she were cold, and began to walk up and down the room.

It was the same pleasant room, with the overstuffed chairs covered in white cretonne, the polished hardwood floor, with rugs scattered on it, which was badly sprung in places and had a tendency to creak near the windows at the back. Vicky looked round the cream-painted walls; at the red-brick fireplace, swept and scrubbed; at the flowers on the grand piano. It was all the same, yet it was all changed.

Because Arthur, *Arthur*, had strangled a girl here. Odd. That was her first thought: the oddness of it. Yet was it so odd? She thought of Arthur: the thick-set figure, the dark complexion, the rare laugh. Pleasant enough, unless you got him out of his intellectual depths. The soul of neatness, and not very liberal with money.

As a lover, she could not get on with him. He was both violent and unskilled. And this prompted dangerous thoughts. In two years of marriage, he had awakened Vicky Fane just enough so that she realized several things. In the proper hands, she realized, she might be . . .

Frank Sharpless's, for instance.

A word to the police—

Vicky shut the thought from her mind. She hated herself for the disloyalty of these thoughts. Arthur was her husband. You could not share the same life, the same house, the same room with a person for two years, twenty-four months, heaven knew how many hours, without conceiving some sort of tolerant liking for him. You had to protect him, whatever happened.

For the life of her, she could not remember now why she had married him. That was all unreal, an engulfed past. At the time he had seemed rather a smoldering, Byronic sort of person; and, as her mother had pointed out, a girl must get married. Dangerous thoughts again, moving through her mind like satyrs.

Once again Hubert Fane cleared his throat.

"My dear," he said with solicitude, "you are not well. This heat is too much for you."

Vicky stopped by the fireplace, and began to laugh hysterically. Hubert shushed her.

"However, since we must pursue this matter, do you mind if I touch on a rather delicate subject?"

"Can you think of any subject more delicate," said Vicky, "than the one we've been talking about?"

"I see no reason," said Hubert, "why this regrettable affair should mar our lives—"

"When every ring at the door-bell may mean—"

Uncle Hubert considered this.

"No, I do not think so. The boy planned with his usual care and thoroughness. But as I was saying. The older you grow, my dear, the more you will come to realize that the secret of a successful life lies in compromise."

"I wish the police thought that."

Hubert was unruffled.

"Now, Arthur appreciates this," he said, not without satisfaction. "And it leads me to my point. I cannot have failed to observe, as a paternal uncle, that your married life with Arthur, though outwardly happy and well-thought-of by the neighbors, has been not without its difficulties."

Vicky did not comment.

"As a young woman, you are, of course, fond of male society." He paused. "Captain Sharpless, for instance."

Vicky stopped short. Her back was towards him, and she was glad of it, for he could not see the color that crept into her face. It was not guilt; it was mortification that this old crook should notice everything. But her wits whirled as well. Was he, she wondered, trying blackmail tactics on *her* now?

"And the same, with regard to the opposite sex," pursued Hubert, "applies to Arthur himself. Have you observed that he appears to find Miss Ann Browning extremely attractive?"

Again Vicky did not comment.

"Well!" said Hubert, twinkling like a benevolent deity. "As the platitude has it, live and let live. With the proper show of discretion on all sides, I see no reason why you should not all be happy without troubling your heads about Polly Allen: a matter which is, after all, best left to the theological authorities. The thing is done. To brood over it now would be both morbid and unprofitable. In fact, I am not sure I cannot find Scriptural authority for this."

Vicky felt rather sick.

"You could find Scriptural authority for anything," she blazed at him, holding to the edge of the mantelpiece and turning round, "you *blackm* . . . !"

"My dear," said Hubert, genuinely concerned, "you must not upset yourself like this. It will be bad for you. And above all things you must look your best, and go on as though nothing had happened. Captain Sharpless and Miss Browning are coming to dinner tonight, I think." He stopped suddenly, reflecting. "Now that I remember it, I took the liberty of inviting a guest of my own."

"Oh, God!"

"Yes. A doctor. A psychiatrist, whose opinion should be of interest to you. Dr. Rich, his name is: Richard Rich. I knew him many years ago, and ran into him this morning in the bar at The Fleece. He has never been a great success in this world. I thought a good dinner might cheer him up." Hubert's eyes were anxious, like those of a well-trained dog. "You don't mind?"

Vicky thought that she was past minding anything.

She walked to the two windows at the back of the room, stopping by one of them to tap her fingers on the sill and stare out into the hot, bright garden. The floor squeaked sharply under her feet there, reminding her that it ought to be seen to; but how did you see to such things?

Her mind hovered round such trifles. An extra guest

for dinner meant rearrangement, and Arthur was a murderer, and at any minute a large policeman might come tapping at the door. Sturdy, well-shaped in her brown jumper and black skirt, with tan stockings and shoes, Vicky stood at the bright window with her head lowered, nagging at herself for disloyal thoughts. Her mind was a bright blank of doubt and misery.

"Uncle Hubert," she said abruptly, "what was she like?"

"Who, my dear?"

"This girl. Polly Allen."

"Now, my dear, I repeat that you must not—"

"What was she *like?*"

"To tell you the truth," Hubert replied, after some hesitation, "she reminded me a little of Ann Browning. Not of Miss Browning's social class, of course; a few years younger, eighteen or nineteen, perhaps; dark hair instead of fair. But with something of the same air about her. Pretty, I should say; though when I saw her last she was no longer pretty."

Vicky clenched her fists. Her thoughts ran round and round again, the same scratchy groove like a caught phonograph needle.

What a situation! What a situation! What a situation!

Two

On the morning of the following day—Wednesday, the twenty-third of August—Mr. Philip Courtney walked out of The Plough Hotel into the sunshine of Regent Street.

Philip Courtney was at peace with all the world.

It was eleven o'clock. He had eaten a late breakfast, smoked the first, most satisfying pipe of the day, and glanced leisurely through the papers. He had nothing on his mind until evening, and an easy job then.

Cheltenham struck him as being as pleasant a town as any in England. He liked its white-painted, geranium-bed dignity; its spacious, shady streets; its suggestion of Bath without the latter town's cramped and dingy lanes. He would go for a stroll before lunch.

And so he was hesitating on the sunny pavement when a voice spoke behind him.

"Phil Courtney! You old horse!"

Courtney turned.

"Frank Sharpless!" he said.

The sight of a khaki uniform was not, in that year nineteen thirty-eight, so frequent in Cheltenham as it is today. Frank Sharpless, a captain in a Sapper regiment, gleamed with all his buttons.

"You old horse!" he repeated. "What are you doing here? On a job?"

"Yes. And you?"

"Leave. I'm visiting my father; he lives here." Sharpless gestured hospitably towards the hotel. "Come in and have one?"

"With pleasure."

In the American Bar upstairs, at a table by the window with pint tankards between them, they regarded each other with real pleasure.

"Phil," said Sharpless, "I'm going to Staff College."

Courtney considered this. "That's good, I suppose?"

"Good?" echoed the other, with hollow incredulity. "It's the biggest damn honor you can get, I'd have you know! I go there next year. Six months, and then anything can happen. I'll probably wind up as a colonel, one day. Can you imagine me as a colonel?" He peered round to look at the three pips on his shoulder-strap, as though trying to envisage what it would look like.

In person Frank Sharpless was a rangy, dark-haired, good-looking fellow, with a real good humor which made him liked everywhere. Also, he had a first-rate mathematical brain. But he did not seem very adept at concealing his feelings. Though he was full of beans this morning, yet he clearly had something on his mind, worrying him.

"Many congratulations," said Courtney, "and all the luck in the world. Cheer-ho."

"Cheer-ho."

"Your father's pleased, I imagine?"

"Oh, pleased as Punch!—Look here, Phil." After taking a deep pull at the tankard, Sharpless set it down abruptly. But he appeared to change his mind again, and edged away from what he had been thinking about. "Still ghosting, are you?"

When it is stated that Philip Courtney was a ghost,

and a real king-specter among ghosts, this means merely that he was a ghost-writer.

He wrote, in short, those autobiographies and reminiscences of well-known persons, eminent, famous, or merely notorious, which the well-known people signed. Phil Courtney was also a conscientious craftsman who really enjoyed his work.

He was a stickler for realism. He tried to make the autobiography of a celebrated harlot sound as though it had actually been written by the celebrated harlot, if she had been endowed with a little—just a very little—more culture and imagination. He tried to make the reminiscences of a sporting peer sound as though they had actually been written by the sporting peer, if he had been endowed with a little—just a very little—more brains. And this pleased everybody.

To him these books were completely satisfying. They represented so many characters he had created, so many personalities of which he was a part, with the advantage over fiction that these characters were real. You could find them in the telephone book or, if sufficiently exasperated by their temperament, kick them in the pants.

Up to this day Phil Courtney, despite minor squalls on the part of his sitters, had been a happy man.

"Still ghosting," he admitted.

"Who is it this time?"

"Quite a bigwig, they tell me. Fellow from the War Office, by the way."

"Oh? What's his name?"

"Merrivale. Sir Henry Merrivale."

Frank Sharpless, who had again lifted the tankard to his lips, slowly set it down untasted.

"You," he said slowly, like one anxious to define the terms carefully, *"you* are going to write the reminiscences of Sir Henry *Merrivale?"*

"Yes. He told the publisher he hadn't time to write

'em himself, but he didn't mind dictating it. Of course that's what a lot of them say, and as a rule it doesn't mean much. I shall have to edit it—"

"Edit it?" roared Sharpless. "You'll have to burn it."

"Meaning what? They tell me he was a big shot during the War, and that he's been mixed up in any number of well-known murder cases."

"And no shadow of doom," said Sharpless, eyeing Courtney with real curiosity in his good-looking, rather fine-drawn face, "no shadow of doom darkens your fair day. No warning voice whispers in your ear: 'Get out of here, and stay out while you've still got your reason.' Well, it won't be long now."

"Here! Oi! What *is* all this?"

"Look here, old boy," said Sharpless, drawing a deep breath and putting his finger-tips on the edge of the table, "I don't want to discourage you. So I will only say this. You are not going to write the reminiscences of Sir Henry Merrivale. You think you are; but you're not."

"Why not? If you mean the old boy's temperamental," smiled Courtney, with the confidence of one whose tact has handled a popular actress and a Russian Grand Duke, "I think I can promise that—"

"Rash youth!" said Sharpless, shaking his head and fixing his companion with a moody eye. "Cripes! Was there ever such rashness?" He frowned. "I didn't know the old boy was down here, though. Where's he staying?"

From his pocket Courtney fished out pipe, pouch, and address book. He lit the pipe and leafed through the book.

"Here we are. 'Care of Major Adams, 6 Fitzherbert Avenue, Old Bath Road, Leckhampton, Cheltenham.' I'm told he first went to Gloucester, to see the Chief

Constable about some criminal business, and then came on here for a rest."

He paused, caught by the expression on Sharpless's face. It was the same expression he had seen there a few minutes ago. Sharpless ran a hand through his dark, wiry hair. Then he clenched his fist, and seemed to meditate hammering it on the table. Instead, after looking round to make sure that the sunlit room was empty except for the barman, he leaned across the table and lowered his voice to a whisper.

"Look here, Phil."

"Yes?"

"That address. Reminds me of some friends of mine. The Fanes. They live close to there."

"Well?"

"Phil, I've gone and fallen for a married woman."

There was a silence.

"No!—strike me blind!" said Sharpless, lifting his right hand as though to take an oath, and drawing back a little. "I mean it. It's serious. It's the real thing."

His voice was still a fierce whisper. Horizontal wrinkles furrowed his forehead.

"But that would . . ." Courtney began. "Staff College," he added warningly.

"Yes! It'd play the devil! Don't I know it? But I can't help it, and that's all there is about it!"

"Who is she?"

"Victoria Fane, her name is. Vicky. They live in Fitzherbert Avenue too. Big, white, square house, set back from the road; you can't miss it as you go by. She's got a swine of a husband who swindles people under the guise of a solicitor. God, Phil, she's *wonderful*. I won't want to bore you with all this . . ."

"You're not boring me. You know that. Go on."

Sharpless drew a deep breath. "I was out there to dinner last night. I'm going again tonight."

"Dinner on two successive nights?"

"Well, there's an excuse. Last night, you see, there were six of us to dinner. Vicky, and this swine Fane—I know I oughtn't to talk about my host like that, but he is a swine and that's all there is to it—and Fane's uncle, and a wishy-washy gal named Ann Browning, and a doctor, and myself. This doctor is one of the kind (what do you call 'em?) who tells you when you've got complexes."

"Psychiatrist?"

"That's it! Psychiatrist. Rich, his name is! Dr. Rich. Well, this Dr. Rich, who's a genial old buffer like John Bull and looks as though he'd got no nonsense about him, started talking about his work. In the course of it he said that he very often used hypnotism."

"Used what?"

"Hypnotism," explained Sharpless, making mesmeric passes in the air by way of illustration.

"Yes?"

"Now, that interested me. I've always thought it was a good deal of a fake. That's to say: I've seen 'em on the stage, where they fetch somebody up out of the audience and make him quack like a duck. But there always seemed to me something very, very phoney about it."

"There's nothing phoney about it, Frank."

"No. That's what Rich told me, and they all backed him up. I'm afraid I got a bit argumentative. I said I didn't maintain it *couldn't* be done; I said all I maintained was that I should like to *see* it done where there was no possibility of a fake.

"I said, furthermore, 'Suppose you could put a person under hypnotic influence like that, so that he or she was absolutely controlled by your will, would that person do anything you ordered?' I was thinking of the dangers of it, you see. I said, 'For instance, could you get a girl to do thus-and-so?' "

Sharpless paused.

He brooded, rubbing the side of his jaw, but with a subdued twinkle in his eye nevertheless. He had a charm of naïveté which enabled him to get away with even worse social bombshells than this.

"It wasn't a very tactful question, I admit," he said.

"Under the circumstances," said Courtney, "perhaps not. Well?"

"Well, Dr. Rich got very grave. He said, yes, you could, if the girl were already inclined that way; and that it was one of the dangers of hypnotism in the hands of unprincipled persons. I saw I'd rather dropped a brick, so I tried to cover it up by saying that what I meant was: could you get her to commit a crime? I said: 'If a victim is really under the will of a hypnotist, wouldn't there be the devil to pay if you told her to commit robbery or murder?' "

Courtney drew at his pipe. "And what did Dr. Rich have to say to that?"

"He explained it. The explanation *sounds* reasonable, I'm bound to admit."

"What is it?"

"That under hypnotism you will only do what you're capable of doing in waking moments. Like this! Suppose Vicky Fane walks into this room now. We hypnotize her, and then say, 'Now walk up to the bar and have a big drink of whiskey.' Vicky doesn't drink much, but she does indulge occasionally. So she'd go and do it like a soldier. You follow that?"

"Yes."

"But suppose you got a real, honest, fanatical teetotaler; a Band-of-Hoper; somebody like Lady Astor, for instance. After hypnotizing her—"

"Beautiful thought."

"Shut up. After hypnotizing her, you plank down half a tumbler of whiskey and say, 'All right, polish that off.' But she wouldn't. She couldn't. She might be in agony, because the hypnotist's will is law. She might even pick up the glass. But she wouldn't. If she did, it would mean there was something wrong with her teetotaler's principles.

"Finally, Dr. Rich said he regretted he hadn't got certain things there that night, or he would show me an interesting experiment which he thought I should find conclusive. That made me suspicious again, and I asked why he couldn't do the experiment now. He said it required certain properties.

"Whereupon Fane's uncle—decent old chap—suggested that we should meet again for dinner the next night, the same lot of us, and Dr. Rich could show us the experiment. Fane, the blister, didn't like this a bit. But I gather that Uncle Hubert is the wealthy relative whom Fane wants to keep on the good side of, so he managed to cough up an invitation. So it's dinner there again tonight."

Again Sharpless paused, uneasily.

"What sort of experiment, Frank?"

"I don't know," admitted Sharpless. His voice was heavy with worry. "Look here, Phil. Would you say that I was what-d'ye-callit? Thingummybob? Psychic?"

Courtney laughed outright.

"All right. Laugh. Your own doom will soon be on you anyhow. But I tell you—" Sharpless brought his fist slowly down on the table—"I tell you there's something funny going on in that house. Under the surface."

Courtney was direct. "You mean you think the lady's husband suspects your intentions?"

Sharpless hesitated, so Courtney prodded again.

"How far has the affair gone?"

"It hasn't gone anywhere yet. Hang it, I haven't even got any reason to suppose she cares two pins for me!" Sharpless brooded. "And yet I do know, too. It was last week. At a damn concert in the Promenade. They were playing *Drink to Me Only with Thine Eyes* ... if you laugh I'll murder you!"

Courtney showed no disposition to laugh. After surveying him narrowly, with defiant embarrassment, Sharpless stared hard at the contents of his tankard and spoke in a muttering voice.

"She doesn't love the swine Fane. That I do know. Not that they don't put up a good front! This Dr. Rich may be hot stuff as a psychologist, but he can't see psychology when it's under his nose. I rode part of the way home with him on the bus last night. And he kept saying what an ideal couple the Fanes were, and how pleasant it was to see such things in this age of divorce, until I could have landed him one."

"H'm."

"But when I say there's something funny going on there, I don't mean *that*, exactly. I mean something else that's queer. And I'm not looking forward to tonight. I wish you could come along."

"I'd like to. But I've got a nine o'clock appointment with Sir Henry Merrivale."

Sharpless moved his shoulders.

"Well?" he said. "You've heard about it now. What's your advice?"

"My advice is: be careful."

"It's all very well to sit there and say that, Phil. But I can't be careful."

"Well, what do you want? Divorce?"

"A divorce, even if Fane consented," said Sharpless, "would mean good-by to the Staff College. But I'm beginning to think—"

"You're beginning to think: never mind the Staff College. To hell with the Staff College. You don't want to go to the place anyway. Is that it?"

"No, not that, exactly. Something like it, though. And, in any case, don't sit there puffing your pipe and looking like the Wise Man of the East. This is serious. I want advice; not sarcasm. Can't you rally round and offer a helpful suggestion?"

Courtney stirred with discomfort. Though he was only half a dozen years older than Sharpless's twenty-seven, he felt at once far older and yet less experienced.

"Look here, Frank. *I* can't solve your problem for you, and neither can anybody else. It's something you've got to work out for yourself."

"Oh, Lord!"

"It's true. If you love this girl, and she loves you, and you can see a way out without too much scandal, I should say go ahead. Have the girl and the Staff College too. Only for the love of Mike make sure you know what you're doing."

Sharpless did not reply.

His shoulders hunched up, and his gaze strayed out of the window down into the street. His eyes, ordinarily gray, were now almost black; the brows pinched together above them.

"That's that, then." He turned round from the window, like a man coming to a decision, and spoke in a different voice. "The governor'll want to see you. What about coming along home with me for lunch?"

"Glad to. But if—"

"No. Let's forget it." Sharpless drained his tankard and got up. "But I wish tonight were over. Cripes, how I wish tonight were over!"

It might have been instinct; it was certainly prophecy. Imperceptibly, a design had now been completed. The arrow was fitted, nock to the string; the bow was drawn to the full arc of its power. You could now only wait for the thud as the shaft went home.

Three

"If everyone is ready," suggested Dr. Richard Rich, "shall we begin the experiment?"

It was nearly nine o'clock. The long, spacious back drawing room was lighted only by a bridge lamp, with a white parchment shade, beside the sofa.

Arthur Fane had always been punctilious about the ceremony of dressing for dinner. But tonight, as a concession to the heat, he had so far unbent as to wear a soft shirt with his dinner jacket. So did the other men with the exception of Frank Sharpless, whose black-and-scarlet mess jacket fitted tightly round the usual stiff shirt and black tie. Vicky Fane wore dark violet, with full skirt and sleeves. Ann Browning was in white. All stood out vividly, even in shadow, against the cream-painted walls.

The windows at the narrow end of the room were open. But their curtains had been partly drawn, so that only the last shreds of daylight entered when Richard Rich took up a position with his back to the red-brick fireplace.

Dr. Rich was a short, stocky, comfortable-looking man in an untidy dinner jacket. He had thrust his hands into the pockets of it. He was bald except for an unexpected brush of hair, black streaked with gray, which began half way down the back of his skull and curled out over his collar. It formed the only vaguely theatrical touch to an otherwise stout, ordinary personality. His round face was slightly flushed with the heat, or with the brandy he had taken after dinner. He was smiling.

"And when we do begin," he continued, softly over a note of heavy brass. "I think Captain Sharpless will understand why I couldn't proceed last night."

Sharpless waved this aside.

"All right. But what is this experiment, exactly?"

"That's what I want to know," agreed Arthur Fane rather sharply. "What are you going to do?"

Dr. Rich smiled in a maddeningly cryptic way.

"With your permission," he said, "I first of all propose to place one of you under hypnosis."

"You're not going to place *me* under hypnosis," said Arthur, "and get me to make a fool of myself in public. Besides, I don't hold with this. It's—it's morbid."

"You would be a bad hypnotic subject anyway," smiled Dr. Rich. "No. With her permission, the person I propose to use for the experiment is Mrs. Fane."

For some reason, this created a minor sensation.

Vicky was sitting bolt upright in a slender chair not far from the fireplace, her hands folded in her lap. She turned her head round, surprised.

"Me?" she asked. "But why? I mean, why me?"

"First, Mrs. Fane, because you're the best hypnotic subject here. The second reason—well, you'll understand the second reason when we have finished."

"But I should have thought . . ."

Vicky did not complete the sentence. What she evidently meant, to judge by the direction of her glance, was that she thought the best subject would be Miss Ann Browning.

Ann Browning was sitting in shadow, in one of the white easy chairs. She bent forward absorbedly, in deep and eager interest. Though about the same age as Vicky, she seemed to have little of the latter's brisk practicality. She was smaller than Vicky, and more slender. Her hair, gold where the light struck it, was bound round her head. Her skin, against the white gown, had merely a clear glow as opposed to Vicky's faint tan.

Dr. Rich's shrewd little eyes interpreted that glance, and answered it.

"You would be wrong, Mrs. Fane," he said.

"Wrong?"

"I suppose you share most people's view that the easiest hypnotic subject is a sensitive or highly strung person? That, as any doctor will tell you, is the exact reverse of true."

Arthur Fane sat up.

"Do you call *me* a sensitive or highly strung person?" he asked incredulously.

"No, Mr. Fane. You are just dogged. You would fight the influence. I doubt whether anybody could hypnotize you."

"By George, you're right there," breathed Arthur. He was flattered and pleased; and, as usual when pleased, his rare, pleasant smile lit up the dark face. He took two puffs at a dead cigar. "But why has it got to be any of us? Why can't we have one of the maids in, and experiment on her?"

"Arthur, they'd talk!" said Vicky warningly.

Her husband saw the justice of this, and subsided. But he did not seem pleased. He kept darting glances, rather hungry glances, in the direction of Ann Browning. Vicky saw these looks too.

"Well, Mrs. Fane?" prompted Rich.

Vicky laughed a little. "I don't mind being the victim, exactly. But it's as Arthur says. I don't want to make a fool of myself in public. This—this is the business where your subconscious mind is supposed to be released, isn't it?"

"Only in a sense. You will be under the control of my will, and must obey my orders."

"Yes, that's what I mean," returned Vicky, rather hastily. "I mean, I shouldn't want to be made to quack like a duck, or go up and kiss somebody, or anything like that."

Throughout the foregoing, Uncle Hubert Fane, who was smoking one of Arthur's best cigars with relish, had several times looked very thoughtful. A watcher might even have said that he seemed apprehensive. Once, at the mention of the subconscious mind, he cleared his throat as though to intervene.

But Dr. Rich forestalled him.

"Mrs. Fane," Rich said gravely, "please remember that this is not a side-show or an exhibition of parlor magic. It is a serious scientific experiment. I'm not even sure that I can bring it off. I give you my word that you will be asked to do nothing which will embarrass you or hold you up to ridicule."

"Come on, Vicky! Be a sport!" urged Ann Browning, in her soft, attractive voice.

"You promise?" Vicky asked Rich.

"I promise."

"All right," said Vicky, lifting her shoulders and smiling not without wryness. "Let the dirty work begin. What do you want me to do?"

There was a general expelling of breaths in the long room.

Rich turned round to the mantelpiece. From the top of it, beside the clock, he took down a cardboard shoe-box which he had long ago placed there in preparation for this.

"Now, Mrs. Fane! First of all, I must tell something to the others which it is necessary that you shall not hear. Would you mind going out into the hall for a moment, until I call you in?"

"What *is* all this?" demanded Sharpless, after a pause. "Charades?"

Rich swung round on him.

"Captain Sharpless, if you will remain silent, and be content to watch an experiment which you yourself challenged me to perform, I think you'll understand what it is in a very few minutes."

"Sorry. No offense intended. But—"

"You don't mind, Mrs. Fane?"

"No, not at all."

Rich had removed the cover from the cardboard box. As Vicky rose to her feet and stepped past him, it was impossible that she should not have at least a brief glimpse inside. Rich replaced the cover on the box rather hastily. Putting it under his arm, he went to open the door for her.

The door was in the same wall as the fireplace: that is, the long wall at right-angles to the windows, but far away from the windows towards the other end of the room.

Rich opened the door for Vicky, stood aside as she went out, and closed it again. It was a good heavy door; but it closed imperfectly and the latch did not catch. As Rich turned back to the others, the door creaked an inch or two open.

Sharpless was about to call his attention to this when the doctor's eye caught them again.

"I have in this box," he said in his soft, heavy bass voice, "two exhibits. Exhibit A—a rubber dagger."

"See here!"—began Arthur Fane.

"Yes?" prompted Ann Browning.

Rich held up the toy dagger. Its blade was painted silvery gray to represent a patchy and unconvincing-looking metal; its handle was black. Without any sense of incongruity, Rich bent the soft rubber back and forth.

"Bought this morning at Woolworth's," he explained. "A sixpenny rubber dagger which can hardly be called dangerous. That's Exhibit A. But Exhibit B is different."

He replaced the dagger in the box, and took out the second article. When they saw it, the breath from his audience was something like a mutter of consternation.

"Exhibit B," said Rich. "A real revolver, loaded with real bullets."

There was a silence.

Over his audience the revolver seemed to exercise a kind of evil fascination. It was a Webley .38, of dark, polished metal except for the ivory grip. Rich broke it open, plucked one of the cartridges from the cylinder, tossed the cartridge into the air, and caught it.

"Definitely not a toy," he pointed out, replacing the bullet and closing the magazine with a sharp click. "In fact, as deadly a weapon as we're likely to find. Therefore . . . yes? Yes? What is it?"

He broke off, frowning at Sharpless.

The latter was going through a pantomime of extraordinary concentration. After screwing up his face and making gestures to attract Rich's attention, Sharpless was stabbing his finger in the direction of the partly open door.

Rich, as though enlightened, uttered an exclamation. He hurried over and closed the door firmly.

"She heard you!" said Sharpless in a whisper. "She couldn't have helped hearing you!"

Rich smiled.

"I sincerely hope she did," he answered with composure. "If she didn't, there is no point in this experiment."

"*What?*"

Rich tossed the pistol across to Sharpless, who automatically caught it.

"Examine that revolver," Rich suggested. "Or, more properly, examine the bullets."

The bullets were dummies.

Each empty brass cartridge-case had been fitted with a little rounded cylinder of wood, painted gray to represent a bullet. Sharpless took out each one in turn, and examined it carefully before he fitted it back again.

"I think I begin to see," he muttered, "what sort of dirty trick you've got in mind. This gun isn't dangerous at all. But—"

"Exactly," agreed Rich. "It is no more a deadly weapon than the dagger. *But Mrs. Fane thinks it is.*"

Uncle Hubert Fane, whose apprehension at first sight of the revolver had now merged into relief, was taking such fast, furious puffs at his cigar that his head appeared to be enveloped in smoke.

"You follow me?" inquired Rich. "Here are two articles. One of them, the dagger, Mrs. Fane's inner mind knows to be harmless. The other, that revolver, she believes to be real. Very well. I shall put Mrs. Fane into a state of hypnosis. Then I shall order her to . . ."

"To kill somebody," breathed Ann Browning.

"Exactly," said Rich.

It was now altogether dark, except for the white light of the parchment-shaded bridge lamp beside the sofa. A faint cooler breeze stirred the curtains at the windows.

"Mind!" added Rich, rubbing a hand vigorously across his bald skull, "I don't say I shall be able to manage this. I may not be able to establish the proper degree of influence. But if I do—"

"If you do?" prompted Ann.

"If I do," smiled Rich, "then I can tell you exactly what will happen. Under hypnosis, you understand, the patient has no mind or will of her own. She is a machine. A zombie. A walking corpse, under my direction. But—"

"Yes?"

"When she is ordered to pick up that revolver and

shoot someone she loves, then she will balk. Even in anguish she won't be able to do it. Powerful as my influence is, it can't get past the barrier in her subconscious mind. But when I order her to take the dagger and stab someone, she will strike without the least hesitation. Because her subconscious mind knows that it's all a game."

Again there was a silence.

"Well, Captain Sharpless?" said Rich. "If I succeed in doing that, will you own yourself convinced?"

"I don't like it!" said that young man abruptly, and jumped to his feet.

"You don't like it, Captain Sharpless? But you were the one who suggested it."

"Yes, but I didn't know what you were going to do. I didn't know you were going to do *this*."

"I think it's the most thrilling thing I've ever heard of," declared Ann Browning.

"Who," asked Sharpless, "who are you going to order her to kill?"

Rich looked surprised.

"Her husband, of course. Who else?"

Frank Sharpless craned his neck round. But if he expected any support from Fane, he did not get it.

From whatever cause, Arthur appeared to have changed his mind. He sat very still in an easy chair, his middle-sized, thick-set figure balanced on the edge of it, staring down at his well-polished shoes. The dead cigar was between his fingers. He moved his heels outwards, a queer gesture, and brought them together again with a click. He glanced up, his dark face impassive.

"I don't hold with this. Still . . . it won't hurt my wife in any way?"

"Oh, no. She may feel tired afterwards. But, if Mrs. Fane is the healthy, uncomplex person I am sure she is, it won't affect her at all."

"Will she know what's happening at the time?"

"No."

"Or remember it afterwards?"

"No."

'Is that so, now?" mused Arthur. He scratched the side of his nose with a fingernail of the same hand that held his cigar. He studied Rich. Again the rare smile gleamed. "Suppose (just suppose, now!) that my wife did have it in her inmost mind to—hurt me?"

Rich was taken aback.

"My dear sir," he began, with the color rising in his face, "I never thought . . . that is, it seemed so obvious! . . . Mr. Hubert Fane assured me . . ."

"Oh, we're only supposing!" Arthur reassured him. He was really smiling now. The thick complacency of his tone would have been felt anywhere, even at his club. "I'm not one to talk about my marriage, as you'll agree. But I don't mind saying that to find a happier couple than Victoria and I you'd have to go far. Very far indeed."

He paused.

"Some people," he added, "might call my life humdrum—"

"Dear boy," interposed Uncle Hubert, with his eye on a corner of the lamp-shade, "I feel sure they would do you no such injustice, if they knew you as I do."

"But *I* don't call it humdrum," concluded Arthur, after giving him a brief look. "Carry on with the experiment."

Frank Sharpless took a few steps up and down the bare hardwood floor, with its few bright rugs. His black mess jacket with scarlet lapels, and close-fitting black trousers with scarlet stripe down the side, gave him a lean and Mephistophelian appearance which was contradicted by the naïve youthfulness of the face. His booted footsteps rattled on the floor. Though he made a gesture of protest, he did not speak again.

"Then we are all agreed?" inquired Rich. "Good!"

He put the lid on the cardboard box containing the revolver and the rubber dagger. This box he handed to Arthur.

"Keep our two exhibits, Mr. Fane, until I tell you what to do with them."

Then Rich went over and opened the door.

"Come in, Mrs. Fane," he invited.

Four

Vicky hesitated in the doorway.

It was as though this were only some guessing-game in which she hesitated about what question to ask first. Her manner indicated this. Yet her tanned, clean-skinned face, the blue eyes more vivid against it, was softened by another underlying emotion. It was fear, and Sharpless knew it.

"Yes?" she said doubtfully.

Rich took her hand. "Come over here, Mrs. Fane, and sit down on the sofa. Make yourself comfortable."

Vicky stopped short.

"I'd rather not sit on the sofa," she said.

Again a brief, vague touch of uneasiness brushed the room.

"Very well, then," agreed Rich, after a slight pause. "We'll try to make you comfortable somewhere else."

He surveyed the room. He walked towards the windows, but there the sharp-squeaking wood of the floor appeared to irritate him. After treading on it experimentally, he turned round and looked at the extreme opposite end of the room. There Arthur Fane was sitting, with the cardboard box on his knees.

"May we have your chair, Mr. Fane?"

Arthur got up.

The bridge lamp had a very long cord. Rich picked it up from beside the sofa, which was pushed back against the long wall opposite the fireplace. He carried the lamp across to the white easy chair where Arthur had been sitting, and tilted its shade to shine down on the chair. He pushed the chair back flat against the wall.

"Will this suit you, Mrs. Fane?"

"Yes, that's all right," said Vicky. She followed him over and sat down.

"That's it. Just relax. The others of you I should like to sit fairly close, but not too close. Draw up your chairs sideways to her, where she can't see you. That's it."

The center of the room was now a cleared space, with Vicky sitting with her back to one wall and facing the windows from some twenty-five feet away. Rich drew the curtains on these windows. In one corner he found a telephone table, round and of polished mahogany. Removing from it the telephone, an address pad, and a cigarette box, he carried this table to the middle of the room, where he set it down.

"Now!" said Rich—and walked back to Vicky.

"Mrs. Fane," he went on, "I want you to put yourself in my hands. I want you to trust me. You do trust me, don't you?"

"Yes, I think I do."

"Very well."

The man's voice was already compelling. It had a musical vibration in its soft bass. Again Rich tilted the shade of the lamp, so that its light shone on his own face. From his pocket he took a coin, a new and polished shilling which shone with bright silver.

"Mrs. Fane, I'm going to hold this a little above the level of your eyes. I just want you to look at it. Look at it steadily. That's all. It will be easy. Do you understand?"

"Yes."

"The rest of you, please be quiet. It is very quiet."

Afterwards, Frank Sharpless was never quite sure how the thing happened.

The room seemed to be full of a soft voice, almost whispering. It went on interminably. It seemed to be leading them past a barrier, into another world. Sharpless could never recall what it said, except that it dealt with sleep, drugging sleep, sleep within dreams, sleep muffled beyond life. It affected even those who were not looking past that bright-shining coin into Rich's eyes.

The clock did not tick; no breath of air stirred in the trees outside; no sense of time existed.

"Sleep now," murmured the voice. "Sleep softly. Sleep deep. Sleep."

And Rich stepped back.

Frank Sharpless felt a chill as though he had been touched with ice.

Vicky Fane lay back quietly, every limb at rest, in the white easy chair. As Rich shifted the light on her, they saw that her eyes were closed. She did not move except for the slow rise and fall of her breast, where the light made a hollow in the smooth flesh above the bodice of the violet-colored gown.

The face, framed in brown bobbed hair, was serene and untroubled, the eyelids waxy, the mouth faintly wistful.

Sharpless, Arthur, Hubert, Ann Browning were all still trying to shake themselves loose from the spell, as from clinging veils on a threshold. Ann spoke, instinctively, in a whisper.

"Can she hear us?"

"No," said Rich, in his normal voice. The change sounded startling. He mopped his moist forehead with a handkerchief.

"Is she really—"

"Oh, yes. She's gone."

"Now, Mr. Fane. Will you take the revolver and the dagger, and place them on that round table I put in the middle of the room?"

Arthur hesitated. For the first time he seemed uneasy. Removing the articles from the cardboard box, he examined them. He bent the rubber dagger back and forth. Suddenly he broke open the magazine of the revolver, drew out and scrutinized each dummy bullet before shutting up the magazine again.

Then, as though sneering at himself, he walked across and put the revolver and dagger on the little table.

He was returning to the group by the easy chair, his footfalls clacking loudly, when they suffered an interruption. The door to the hall opened. Daisy the maid, put her head in.

"Please, sir—" she began.

Arthur turned on her.

"What the devil do you mean by coming in here?" he demanded. His normal voice sounded loud, hard, and harsh against the still-clinging quiet. "I told you—"

Daisy shied back, but stuck it out. "I couldn't help it, sir! There's a man outside, asking for Mr. Hubert, and he won't go away. He says his name's Donald MacDonald. He says—"

Arthur turned to Hubert.

"Is that . . ." Arthur swallowed, but was compelled to complete the sentence. "Is that your bookmaker again?"

"I regret, my dear boy," Hubert conceded, "that such appears to be the fact. Doubtless Mr. MacDonald will be forgiven his sins in a better world (including, let us hope, his avarice), but at the moment I fear he is vulgar enough to want money. A slight miscalculation on my part, despite information straight from the stable—"

"Then go and pay him off. I won't have such people seen at my house, do you hear?"

"Unfortunately, my boy, I have just remembered that I failed to go to the bank today. The sum is trifling: five pounds. If you would be kind enough to advance it to me until tomorrow morning?"

Arthur breathed through his nostrils, heavily. After a pause he reached into his pocket, drew out a notecase, counted out five pound notes, and handed them to Hubert.

"Until tomorrow, my boy," promised Hubert. "I shall be back in a moment. Pray continue the experiment."

The door closed after him.

The spell, which should have been broken, was not broken at all. It may be doubted whether anybody except Arthur had even noticed this byplay. Sharpless, Ann Browning, even Rich himself were gathered round Vicky, regarding her with emotions which need not be described. Arthur Fane spoke quietly.

"And now what?"

"Now," said Rich, mopping his forehead again before putting away the handkerchief, "comes the most difficult part. You have had your breather. Now sit down again, and don't move or speak again until I give you leave. It may be dangerous. Is that clear?"

"But—"

"Please do as I ask."

Two chairs were drawn up on either side of Vicky, ahead and a little in front of her. Sharpless and Ann Browning sat at one side. Arthur sat at the other side, near the empty chair which had been Hubert's. Dr. Rich stood in the midst of this semi-circle, facing Vicky. He allowed the silence to lengthen again before he spoke.

"Victoria Fane," he said softly. The same eerie voice

froze them again. "You hear me. You hear me, but you will not yet awake."

He paused.

"Victoria Fane, I am your master. My will is your law. Now speak. Repeat after me: 'You are my master, and your will is my law.' "

It was as though the voice had to travel a long way. After perhaps three seconds, the dummy figure in the chair stirred. A shiver went through Vicky's body. Her head rolled a little to one side. Her lips moved.

" 'You are—' " Everyone jumped when she spoke. It was a whisper; it was not even Vicky's voice; it was like a grotesque echo of the voice which had begun to cut away her soul. " 'You are my master,' " it whispered, " 'and your will is my law.' "

" 'Whatever I am asked to do, that I will do without question. For this is for my own good.' "

The figure in the chair struggled, and became limp.

" 'Whatever I am asked to do,' " it replied colorlessly, " 'that I will do. For this is for my own good.' "

" 'Without question!' "

" 'Without—question.' "

Rich drew a deep breath.

"Now you will awaken," he said. "Open your eyes. Sit up. Gently now."

"*God!*" cried Sharpless involuntarily.

Rich's fierce gesture silenced him; the brief glance Rich gave over his shoulder kept him silent.

The person looking back at them from the chair was not Vicky Fane. At least, it was not any Vicky Fane they had ever known. From her eyes, even from her whole face, all those qualities which render a face recognizable as human—intelligence, will, character—had all been drained away. It breathed, and it was warm; but it remained clay. In that utter lack of intelligence, even her good looks seemed to have disappeared.

Vicky sat up quietly, without curiosity. She did not blink in the light.

"I warned you," muttered Rich, moistening his lips. "Now watch."

He spoke to his victim.

"On the floor over there by the window, where I put them when I moved the telephone table," he said, "you will find a cigarette box and a box of matches. Bring me a cigarette and a match."

Arthur Fane began, "There's no match b—" But again Rich's glance imposed silence.

The animal in the chair got to her feet.

She walked straight ahead of her. Without looking at it, she passed the little round table which held the revolver and the dagger.

It was darkish at the other end of the room. Reaching the windows, she bent down. She seemed to peer and grope, searching. She pounced on the silver cigarette box, took a cigarette out of it, and pushed it aside. Then she searched for the box of matches; the high heels of her slippers creaked and cracked on the bad flooring as she searched. The seconds lengthened. From Vicky Fane came suddenly a little moaning cry.

"She can't find it, you see," said Rich.

"This is plain cruelty," said Sharpless, who was white to his lips. "I won't have it any longer."

"*You* won't have it, Captain Sharpless?" inquired Arthur.

"Never mind the matches. You needn't bring me a match," said Rich. His voice was soothing. It reached out softly across the room. It seemed to draw a blanket of warmth round her shoulders as she stood trembling. "Bring me the cigarette instead."

Vicky did so.

Rich looked at the grand piano in the corner by the windows.

"She plays?" Rich asked Arthur.

"Yes, but—"

"Sit down at the piano," Rich instructed softly. "You are happy, my dear. Very happy. Play something. Sing or hum it as you do, to show us you are happy."

Something was wrong again. Vicky's fingers rested on the keys of the piano. The piano was in gloom; Vicky's back was turned to them some distance away. Yet she seemed to be struggling with herself.

"I command you, my dear. Play anything. Any—"

The piano tinkled, and its keys ran softly.

> *"Drink to me only with thine eyes,*
> *And I will pledge with mine;*
> *Or leave a kiss within the cup,*
> *And I'll not ask for wine. . . .*
> *The thirst—"*

The voice, which had been trying to hum raggedly, broke off in a sob.

"That will be enough," Rich said quickly.

His expression changed. It was now very grave. Rich's eyes, now grown sharp and shrewd and suspicious, moved round the group. He ran a hand across his bald skull, down to the roll of gray-streaked hair over his collar. He was human again, and very much troubled.

"Gentlemen," he said, "gentlemen, I think I've been in danger of making a grave mistake. I should not have consented to do this until I—investigated. Has Mrs. Fane any association with that particular song?"

"Not that I know of," replied Arthur, with dreary surprise. "Unless, of course, Captain Sharpless can tell us?"

Rich glanced at Sharpless's face.

"I think we had better end this."

"And I think not," said Arthur Fane.

"You insist on that, sir?"

"You, sir, promised to show us something. You have not yet done so."

"As you like," breathed Rich. "Sit down again, then." He waited until the three spectators had done so. "Victoria Fane, walk up to the table in the middle of the room. On that table you will find a loaded revolver. Pick it up."

In the group, it was as though nobody dared to draw his breath. Ann Browning, who had not uttered a word, was bending forward with her knees crossed and her slim hands gripped round them. Her gold hair caught the light. The color in her cheeks, the brilliant shining of her pale blue eyes, made a contrast to the shabby, tear-streaked face of the automaton.

"Walk forward until I tell you to ... there! Stop! Now turn to your right a little more—facing your husband."

Arthur Fane moistened his lips.

"Stand back a few steps ... that's it. *Captain Sharpless, if you touch Mrs. Fane in any way, you may do her a serious injury.*"

Sharpless jerked back.

"Victoria Fane, you hate the man sitting in front of you. He has done something which you consider unforgivable. You hate him from the bottom of your heart. You wish him dead."

Vicky did not move.

"You hold a loaded revolver. From where you stand, it would be easy to shoot him through the heart. Look."

From his inside pocket Rich took out a pencil of soft, dark, rather smeary lead. He went up to Arthur, and, before the latter could protest, he drew a cross on the left breast of his host's soft shirt.

"There is his heart. Higher up than you thought it was. You wish him dead. I order you to kill him. I will count three, and then you will fire. One ... two ..."

If the hammer fell on even a dud cartridge, it would make a sharp click. Every ear strained for that click.

Vicky's finger, shaking like the whole movement of her arm and shoulder and body, did not tighten. It loosened and uncurled from the trigger. The revolver dropped with a crash and clatter on the hardwood floor.

She could not do it.

Dr. Richard Rich, expelling his breath slowly, closed up his eyes with relief. It was a second or two before he could smile again.

Though he remained impassive, Arthur Fane could not help the flicker of a complacent smirk which crossed his face. He tried to look cool and unconcerned, yet the other expression intruded, welling up from deep in vanity.

"Ah!" smiled Rich. "You refuse to use the revolver, then. But perhaps it isn't suited to you. Perhaps you can force yourself to use a dagger. A dagger is a woman's weapon. There is a dagger on the table. Get it."

Rather unsteadily, Vicky moved towards the table.

"Good. Pick it up. Grasp the handle firmly. Now return here, and . . . stop."

He shaded his eyes with his hand.

"Your hate for the man in front of you is increased. The weapon you hold is just as deadly as the revolver. There is his heart. Strike."

Without hesitation Vicky lifted her arm and struck like a snake.

Grandly, like a satisfied showman, Dr. Richard Rich turned round on his heel to look at Sharpless and Ann Browning. He was smiling. His hand was extended, palm upwards, like one who says, "Well?"

But he did not say it.

Behind him, the door to the hall opened. Hubert Fane, effulgent and self-satisfied, opened the door; and then stopped short. Rich saw the expression on his face as Hubert stared from behind Sharpless and Ann Browning, beyond them to Arthur.

And Rich himself whirled round.

Arthur Fane coughed only once. A black handle, which looked like rubber but could not have been rubber, was protruding from Arthur's white shirt just over the cross Rich had drawn there. But the shirt was no longer white. A moving stain, dull red, widened and deepened round the handle as its edges soaked through the thin fabric.

Arthur, his elbows dug into the arms of the chair, tried to push himself forward. His knees shook. His lips drew back, writhing, for what must have been a second of intense agony. Then he pitched forward on his face.

Five

Nobody moved. It may be accounted as doubtful whether anybody could have moved. Such a sight as this had first of all to be understood.

The seconds ticked by: ten, twenty, thirty. Arthur Fane lay partly on his side and partly on his face, also without moving. The light of the lamp was reflected in patches from the polished hardwood floor.

Presently, Dr. Rich went down on one knee beside Arthur. He rolled Arthur over on his back. First he felt for a pulse at the wrist; then he took his watch out of his pocket, and held it so that the crystal almost touched Arthur's lips. No breath clouded the glass. After consulting the watch as to the time, Rich replaced it in his pocket.

"Incredible as it seems, this man is dead."

"Dead?" echoed Sharpless.

"Dead. Stabbed through the heart."

"Oh, no," said Hubert Fane. "No, no, no, no, no!"

Uncle Hubert's tone, at the moment, was merely one of frightened skepticism. His manner indicated that the world couldn't play him a dirty trick like this.

"No, really, now!" he said, as though determined to stop such nonsense at once. "This is too much. I must really protest. Get up, my dear boy! Get up and—"

"He won't hear you," said Rich, as Hubert began to chafe at one of Arthur's wrists. "I tell you he's dead."

Then Rich reached out and touched the black handle projecting from Arthur's chest. He pressed it between his fingers.

"And I'll tell you something else," he added, his color going up. *"That's not the dagger I brought to this house."*

"I shouldn't touch it, if I were you," warned Sharpless. "The police always kick up a row if you mess about with the evidence. At least, they do in the stories. Don't touch it!"

"But why not?" asked Ann Browning. "After all—we know who stabbed him, don't we?"

For the first time they felt the full shock.

Vicky Fane was standing quietly a few feet away from the man she had killed. Her hands hung down at her sides. She was not looking at him, or at anything else. The sight of that witless creature, with intellect removed and eyes as dead as blue china, where formerly there had been a vital, laughing, attractive girl, was almost too much for Frank Sharpless. The grimy marks of tears still streaked her cheeks, though she showed no emotion now.

"Dr. Rich," said Sharpless, "the celebrated Dr. Frankenstein had nothing on you."

Rich put his hands to his forehead.

"Don't wake her up!" snapped Sharpless, misinterpreting the gesture. "For God's sake don't wake her up!"

"I wasn't going to wake her up, young man."

"Can she hear us?"

"No."

"But even if you don't wake her up"—Sharpless swallowed hard—"can't you *do* something?"

"Yes. One moment." Rich turned to Vicky. His voice

was slow and heavy. "Victoria Fane, go over to the sofa. Put a pillow under your head. Lie down."

With instant obedience Vicky went to the sofa. She shuddered violently as she touched it, and Rich was after her in an instant. He put his fingers lightly on her temples; the shuddering died away, and she lay down.

"Now sleep," murmured Rich, in the voice that could influence them all. "You are yourself again, Victoria Fane. But sleep. You will not awaken until I tell you to. When you wake up, you will have forgotten everything that happened here. Now sleep. Sleep . . ."

Sharpless hurried to her side. And in a moment or two he breathed something like a strangled prayer.

It was like watching a blurred image come into focus, or cold clay warmed again with humanity. Something (mind? heart? soul?) seemed to flow into her, altering even the lines of the face. Vicky Fane lay where the dummy had lain, the smudged marks of the tears incongruous on her cheeks.

Her color was back, the faint tan of health, the familiar curve of the lips. Her breathing was slow and easy, and she smiled in sleep.

"Thank . . . *God*. If anybody ever does that to her again—"

Rich looked round.

"Captain Sharpless, has Mrs. Fane any unpleasant mental association with this sofa?"

"I'll swear *I* don't know."

"Mr. Hubert Fane, has she any unpleasant mental association with this sofa?"

"My dear doctor, you must not ask me." For all his elegance and poise, Hubert's complexion was muddy gray under the gray-white hair. "I can scarcely imagine that an inanimate piece of furniture could so affect anybody. Does—does the girl know what has happened?"

"No," snapped Rich. "Do you?"

"I'm beginning to think I do," said Sharpless.

"Yes. And I," agreed Rich. "Somebody switched the daggers. Look here."

Again he knelt beside Arthur's body. With some difficulty, and despite an instinctive protest from everyone, he pulled the weapon out of the wound. Since the heart had stopped pumping, only a little blood followed it.

It was a knife made of very light, very thin steel, with a blade perhaps four inches long. When Rich cleaned it on a handkerchief, they saw that the blade had been painted over a dirty silver-gray. A covering of soft black rubber had been gummed round and over what was presumably a very thin handle.

Moved a little away from the light, it looked very much like the rubber dagger they had seen.

"I thought so," said Rich. "Thick rubber round the handle. And it's pretty dark by that little table. When Mrs. Fane picked it up, she felt the rubber and even her subconscious mind told her it was the same toy dagger she expected it to be. So she didn't hesitate to obey the order." He balanced the knife in his palm. "Even the weight wouldn't tell her any different. Somebody's got a lot to answer for."

"You mean—"

"I mean," said Rich, putting the knife on the floor and getting up, "that *I* can't be held responsible. Not this time. Someone exchanged a harmless dagger for a real one, and got Mrs. Fane to kill her husband without knowing what she was doing." He pressed a hand to his pink forehead. "It's odd. It's devilish odd. We know the murderer. But we don't know the guilty person."

There was a silence.

"But how could anybody have exchanged the daggers?" wondered Ann Browning.

"Eh?"

"I said," repeated Ann in a small but clear voice, "how could anybody have exchanged the daggers?"

They all turned to look at her.

For the first time they became conscious of her as a personality, because in these events she had (they remembered) not cried out, or whimpered, or fainted, or done anything they might have expected.

She was rather pale, and she had pushed her chair farther back from Arthur's body: no more. Her slim fingers plucked at the arms of the chair.

"You see—" She stopped as though confused, but presently went on. "The last person to touch the dagger was Mr. Fane himself. Wasn't it?"

Again there was a silence.

"It was," Sharpless said abruptly.

"He was sitting there," pursued Ann, puckering up her face, "with the revolver and the dagger in his hands. It was a rubber dagger then. Because I remember him twisting it back and forth."

The memory of everyone present moved back into the past, recalling images.

"That's true," admitted Rich, with the same abruptness. "I saw him do it myself."

"Then *you*—" Ann looked at Rich—"told him to put the revolver and the dagger on that little table. He got up, and went to the table, and put them down, and came back here. *But not one of the rest of us has been anywhere near that table since.*"

The recollection was so clear, the fact so undeniable, that no one spoke. They all turned to look at the table, which was in the middle of the room at least twelve feet away from the huddled group round the easy chair.

Ann hesitated, moistening her pink lips.

"Please. I don't want you to think I'm intruding, or speaking up when I shouldn't. But look.

"None of us left this semi-circle where we were

standing or sitting. We stayed where we were, even when Vicky was out of the circle herself and going to the other end of the room. Dr. Rich didn't follow her: he stayed here too. We could all see each other all of the time. Nobody went near that table. None of us could have exchanged the daggers."

Once more the long pause stretched out. . . .

"That's true!" Sharpless exploded. "It's as true as gospel!"

Rich managed a smile, a heavy, uneasy twist of a smile.

"You're quite a detective, Miss Browning," he observed, and the color rose in her face. "I can't help agreeing. It is true. And in that case . . ."

Ann frowned.

"Well, you see, in that case it means that somebody who wasn't in the room must have sneaked in and—"

She paused. As her eyes moved round, they rested on Hubert Fane; and her expression became frightened.

"So," observed Dr. Rich thoughtfully.

Hubert Fane had one hand on the back of a chair. He looked like a man on whom the fates are playing dirty tricks much faster and more unreasonably than any human being ever deserved.

"Please don't think—!" began Ann.

Hubert cleared his throat.

"Your delicacy, Miss Browning," he said, "fills me with ecstasy. At the same time, I am capable of taking a hint. Madam, I did not kill my nephew. I think I can give you my solemn assurance that he was the last person in the world I wished to see dead. It is true that I was obliged to leave the room. But, apart from the fact that I was talking to a grasping bookmaker named—"

"Wait!" urged Ann.

She put her finger-tips to her forehead.

"You don't mind?" she asked Hubert.

Hubert gestured the courteous assent of a man who, privately, would like to put her across his knee and wallop her.

"You couldn't have exchanged those daggers before you went out of the room," said Ann. "Because the same thing applies to you as applies to the rest of us. You never went near that table at any time. When you were called out of the room, I remember watching you. You never left the semi-circle before you walked straight out of the room after Daisy."

"That also," agreed Sharpless, "is true."

"Sir. Madam. I thank you. But—"

"But," said Ann, "I don't see how you—oh, please!—you or anybody else could have got in here to do it afterwards. Or to do it at any time, if it comes to that."

Dr. Richard Rich appeared to be considerably taken aback by the rush with which this quiet girl had gathered up the proceedings in her own hands.

"Nobody could have got in at any time? I don't follow that."

"Well . . . for instance, the door."

"Yes?"

"It's almost on top of us," said Ann. "It creaks badly no matter how you try to open it. Could anyone have come in there, walked past the light clear across to that table on a bare hardwood floor, changed the daggers, and walked out again, without our seeing him?"

They envisaged this.

"No," said Sharpless. "It's impossible. Besides, I'll swear nobody did."

Rich massaged his head. "But the windows?" he suggested.

"That floor!" cried Ann. "And the drawn curtains! And—"

With a cluck of his tongue as though in realization, Sharpless strode across to the windows. As soon as he reached the section of the floor anywhere near the windows, the resulting creaks and cracks made him pause.

He looked at the white curtains, smoothly drawn and undisturbed. He pushed them aside on one window, and put his head out.

"This window," he reported, "is eight feet up from the ground. Has anybody got an electric torch?"

Hubert Fane fetched one out of a drawer in the telephone table. Sharpless switched it on, and swept its beam outside.

"Eight feet up," he said, "and there's an unmarked flower-bed underneath. Nobody even climbed up here, much less disturbed those curtains, climbed in, and got twelve or fifteen feet across hell's own squeaky floor to the table—all without being seen or heard. It's just impossible. Come and look for yourselves."

He switched off the torch. He turned round from the window and ran a hand through his hair. The tall black-and-scarlet devil seemed to have become a much bewildered and harassed young man.

"But *we* didn't do it," he protested.

"No." Rich's voice was sharp. "We can be certain we didn't do it. Any of us. We can—what's the word?—give each other an alibi."

"But somebody changed the daggers!"

"How?" asked Ann.

"You don't suppose—" Sharpless hesitated—"you don't suppose Fane did it himself?"

"When," inquired Rich, "he knew he was going to be stabbed with it? And, in fact, insisted on this when I wanted to stop the experiment?"

They looked at each other.

Rich fastened the button of his shabby dinner jacket, and squared his shoulders. Though he seemed the most disquieted person there, you would also have said that he was the most resolute.

"I'm afraid we can't stop here arguing," he declared. "Whether we like it or not, we've got to call in the police. I suggest that we delegate one of us to ring up now, and try to explain what happened. It won't be easy."

"*I'll* ring the police, if you like," offered Ann Browning.

Again they turned to stare at her, and she lowered her eyes.

"You see," she explained hesitantly, "I—I live in Cheltenham. But I work in Gloucester. I'm the Chief Constable's, Colonel Race's, private secretary. I know a little about these things, because Colonel Race sometimes takes me along with him. He says I can get things out of the women."

She made a deprecating grimace with her lips.

"So I thought perhaps if I could get in touch with Colonel Race himself, it might help. But still, maybe it would be better if a man did it. Do you think so?"

Rich regarded her with deepening interest. Even Frank Sharpless pricked up his ears, as though he had never noticed the girl before. Hubert Fane's expression was one of mild pride.

"My dear young lady," Rich told her with some fervor, "the job is yours. There's the telephone. Go to it. But what in the name of sanity are you going to tell them?"

Ann bit her lip.

"I don't know," she confessed. "It may be rather nasty for us. Especially if they call in Scotland Yard: as they probably will, because Colonel Race won't like his own people making awkward situations here. But there you are. You see, I'm *certain* none of us did it. But—"

It was Sharpless who finished this for her.

"But," he said rather wildly, "you're just as sure about the other thing. So am I. I've got eyes. I've got ears. I'll take my Bible oath, I'll swear to my dying day, that nobody could have got in here either by the windows or by the door!"

And, as a matter of fact, he was perfectly right.

Six

In the library of a house not far away, Sir Henry Merrivale was beginning to dictate his memoirs.

It was an impressive moment. H.M., his spectacles down on his nose and his bald head glistening, was piled somehow into the desk chair in the room whose walls were hung with his host's collection of old weapons. H.M. had assumed what he believed to be an impressive posture: his elbow on the desk, and one finger at his temple like Victor Hugo. He tried to refrain from looking pleased with this, and merely succeeded in looking stuffed.

"I was born," he began, with suitable portentousness, "on February 6, 1871, at Cranleigh Court, near Great Yewborough, in Sussex."

This, Philip Courtney thought, was going to be easy.

Courtney had spent a lazy afternoon. He strolled along the Promenade. He had coffee at the Cavendish. He tasted the "waters," and visited the museum. Towards nine o'clock, after a late dinner, he boarded a number three bus at the Center and was put down by the conductor at the beginning of Fitzherbert Avenue.

Yet he remained uneasy.

There were only half a dozen houses in the avenue, each set back in its own grounds behind shoulder-high stone walls. As he passed the big white square house which must belong to Arthur Fane, he stopped and looked at it.

No lights showed at the front. The summer dusk lay warm on quiet trees.

He wondered how Frank Sharpless was getting on, and how love-affairs could so play the devil with a man's mentality. But he had little time to wrestle with this. At the last house in the road—with the Cotswolds looming behind it—he was greeted by Major Adams, who passed him on to the library.

Here he was met by Sir Henry Merrivale with a violent handshake but a glare of such active malignancy that Courtney hurriedly thought back over recent events, wondering what the man could have heard against him. It presently struck him, however that this must be part of H.M.'s normal social manner; for he could tell that his host was trying to be affable. At all events, H.M. settled down at the desk, assumed his heroic pose, and indicated that he was ready to begin.

"Yes, sir?"

H.M. cleared his throat.

"I was born," he said with suitable portentousness, "on February 6, 1871, at Cranleigh Court, near Great Yewborough, in Sussex. My mother was formerly Miss Agnes Honoria Gayle, daughter of the Rev. and Mrs. William Gayle, of Great Yewborough. My father—notwithstandin' the slanderous rumors circulated at the time—was Henry St. John Merrivale, eighth baronet of the name."

Courtney made a slight noise.

"Have you got that down?" inquired H.M., peering over his spectacles.

"Yes, sir. But are you sure that's quite the way you want to begin?"

The corners of H.M.'s mouth drew down.

"What's wrong with it?" he demanded sternly. "Who's writin' this book, you or me?"

"I only thought it might be more—"

"You let me alone, son," H.M. urged, with an air of darkly sinister things hidden. "I know what I'm doin'. I got my reasons for usin' just exactly those words. Burn me, if I don't do anything else in this book, I *am* goin' to right a few old misunderstandings and settle a few old scores. Are you goin' to take down what I say, or not?"

"Right-ho. Fire away."

H.M., ruffled, settled down to resume his interrupted train of thought.

"These rumors," he continued, "were deliberately circulated by my father's second brother, George Byron Merrivale, who may be described with moderation as a bounder and a louse. I will give my readers some idea of this man's character.

"He was warned off the Turf in 1882; kicked out of Boodle's for cheating at cards in the following year; married, sometime in the nineties—I disremember when—Sophy Treliss, because she was supposed to have money; and died of cirrhosis of the liver in 1904, leaving two sons, Robert Blandforth Merrivale and Hugo Parr Merrivale, who now run a bucket-shop in the City and are almost as crooked as he was."

"*No,*" said Courtney, whacking the edge of the little table at which he had been set to take down the great man's reminiscences.

"Oh, for the love of Esau what's wrong *now?*"

"Libel."

"Nonsense. You can't libel a dead man."

"Yes, but these two sons aren't dead. Or at least you say they're not."

H.M. considered this. "You think maybe it's a bit strong."

"Strong? It'll get you a thousand-pound suit for damages before you're even out of the first paragraph."

"Well . . . now," H.M. reflected again. "Yes, maybe it is a bit on the outspoken side. All right. I'll tell you what we'll say. We'll say, 'Robert Blandforth Merrivale and Hugo Parr Merrivale, who are now in business in the City and have inherited many of the family traits.' *That's* all right, surely?"

"But—"

"I didn't say their *father's* traits. I said the family traits. Lord love a duck, sayin' they've inherited the family traits is practically praising 'em, ain't it?"

Though Courtney seemed to detect a flaw in this argument, he remained silent.

"I will now give a sketch of my childhood days," he continued abruptly. "These childhood days would have been pleasant enough had they not been poisoned by the aforementioned George Byron Merrivale.

"This weasel was always the first to insist that I should be sent to the dentist or have my hair cut. He 'heard my lessons' by asking me what was the capital of Bessarabia, or setting sums in arithmetic about the activities of a half-witted goop who was always goin' into a provision-merchant's and ordering enough groceries to last the average family for the next fourteen years.

"If I got the answer wrong, which I generally did, he would turn to my father and say, 'Henry, that boy's not being brought up right.' Then I got walloped because I wasn't being brought up right. Was this justice?"

H.M. gave the last sentiment a powerful oratorical flourish, and eyed his listener as though he expected an answer.

But he fell to brooding again.

"However, I am happy to say that life for George Byron Merrivale was not all ginger-pop either. At the age of eighteen months, when I first remember seein' him, I howled my head off. At the age of three I bit his finger almost through. At the age of five I poured hot treacle in his hat. But at the age of seven I fixed the bounder good and proper. I will now tell my readers how I did this."

An expression of secret glee stole over H.M.'s face.

"You're gettin' all this down, are you?" he inquired anxiously.

"I am."

"Every word of it?"

"Every word of it. But are you sure your memory goes back as far as the age of eighteen months?"

"Oh, I was somethin' of a prodigy," H.M. admitted, not without complacency, "but I was tellin' you about the measures I took for dealin' with my Uncle George."

Again he assumed the stuffed air which indicated that he was now dictating.

"I unscrewed the big mirror from over my mother's dressing table. I took this out on the roof, among the chimneys, on a fine sunny day when I knew George Byron Merrivale would be driving along the road in his fine trap. I caught the reflection of the sun in the four-foot mirror, and I sent the beam from it smack into his eyes."

(Courtney tried to picture his host, as a malignant small boy in large spectacles, sitting cross-legged among the chimneystacks with the mirror.)

"The louse had to pull up. He couldn't move. Forward, sideways, or back, wherever he tried to go I kept him blinded. This did not please him. Always noted for the vileness of his language, he now outdid himself. I could endure this no longer. Revolted by the bastard's profanity, I moved my mirror and sent its beam straight into the off-side eye of the horse."

"Of the what?"

"Of the horse," said H.M., coming off his dignity suddenly and just as suddenly resuming his pose again.

"This was effective. The noble animal took fright and bolted down the road at a speed only equaled by George Merrivale himself when pursued by his creditors. George Merrivale, taken off guard, went behind-over-ears into the road.

"He was not, I assure my readers, hurt in the least. Yet for this innocent escapade, which they will agree could've offended nobody with a sense of humor, I was chased three times round the stables before receivin' the worst walloping I had ever got prior to this date. Was *that* justice?"

He paused.

"Candidly," replied Courtney, since an answer seemed to be expected of him, "I should say yes."

"Oh? You think so, hey?"

"If you don't mind plain speaking, I should say you must have been as villainous a little thug as ever walked."

"Oh, I was no mollycoddle," said H.M., obscurely pleased. He stuck his thumbs into the armholes of his waistcoat.

"I will now deal with the time I put shaving-cream in George Merrivale's alarm-clock, so that every time the alarm rang the clock started to froth like a beer-tap. Or perhaps it will interest my readers more to hear—"

"Excuse me, sir. But did you ever devil anybody except your Uncle George?"

"How do you mean?"

"Well, I want to get the thing in perspective, that's all. If you go on like this, your readers will expect you to be giving him poison by the age of fifteen."

"To tell you the truth," nodded H.M., "I thought of doin' that. I disliked that blister then, and I dislike him yet. This is doing me a lot of good, son. Haah! When I begin—"

"And do you date your first interest in crime from that time?"

H.M. looked blank.

"Crime?"

"I mean your success in solving criminal cases, both connected with the War Office and outside it?"

"Oh, son!" said H.M., shaking his head dismally and directing a pitying glance at his visitor. "There's nothing in that."

"No, sir?"

"No. Lemme tell you so about some of the *real* things. I can't be bothered with these criminal cases any more. They don't interest me. I wouldn't touch one if—"

"Telephone for you, sir," interrupted a lean and elderly maid, sticking her head into the room.

"Hey?"

"Gloucester wants you. Office of the Chief Constable, that's what they say."

H.M. glowered at his guest with a look of deep, challenging suspicion, but Courtney kept a guileless face. H.M. cursed telephones and Chief Constables. But he plodded out into the hall to take the call. Courtney could hear him bellowing to the instrument like a sergeant-major on a parade-ground.

"Looky here, Race. I *told* you the cyanide was in the knitting-bag, and if you arrest that sister-in-law . . ."

Pause.

"What do you mean, another case? . . .

"Race, I tell you I can't! Burn me, I got important work on hand. I'm dictatin' my . . .

"Well, if you think it's goin' to be embarrassing, why don't you call in Scotland Yard? . . .

"Oh, you're going to? Then why bother me? . . .

"What do you mean, another 'impossible' situation? ..."

The telephone appeared to be speaking at length.

"Is that so, now? ...

"And what's the name of this bloke who's been murdered? ...

"Spell it. Oh! Fane! Arthur Fane."

Philip Courtney jumped to his feet. The pipe he had been filling dropped out of his hands on the table.

He had been through a variety of emotions in the past hour. First there had been the necessity to keep a straight face, and refrain from laughing into H.M.'s empurpled visage.

Second, it seemed to him that a man must be dead and buriable who could not find pleasure in these memoirs, provided Courtney himself didn't go mad first and provided libel, scandal, and scurrilousness could be reduced to a minimum.

But now—

Again he listened as H.M.'s voice bellowed out.

"All right, all right, all *right!* Looky here, Race. I'll do it on one condition. The chap you want from London is called Masters. Chief Inspector Masters. ...

"Yes, that's it. You get him into this hot water, and I'll jump in too. ...

"I can depend on that, can I? ...

"All right, then. Yes, I'll go over now, if you're so blinkin' hot about it. All right. Hoo-hoo. G'-by."

The receiver went up with a bang.

When H.M. plodded back into the library, he wore a somewhat guilty air which he tried to conceal under a truculent scowl. His corporation, ornamented by a large gold watch-chain, was truculent of itself.

"Get your hat, son," he said. "You're comin' along."

"Where?"

"Just up the road," insisted H.M., his truculence

changing to honeyed persuasion. "A solicitor named Arthur Fane has been polished off by his wife—"

"God Almighty!"

"But there seems to be some doubt about who did it." All of a sudden Courtney was conscious of sharp little eyes boring into him from behind the spectacles; they made him jump.

"What's the matter, son?" asked H.M. casually. "You don't know anything about it, do you?"

"No, but this autobiography—"

"Napoleon," said H.M., "could do five or six things at once. I can have a good shot at managin' two. You come along. I'll sort of look into this; and at intervals I'll sort of dictate to you over my shoulder."

Courtney, on the point of intimating that this was the craziest idea which even H.M. appeared to have had so far, checked himself and thought of Frank Sharpless. After all, why not?

"But I can't go barging in there!"

"You can," replied H.M. simply, "if you're with me. Colonel Race says his secretary's there. Gal named Ann Browning. Race says this gal's got her headpiece screwed on right, and knows a thing or two. That's all eyewash, naturally. There never was a woman who was any ruddy good as a secretary; except my Lolly-pop, of course, and she's different. But it might be interestin' to see what this gal says."

"Well—"

"Get your hat," glared H.M., "and come on."

Courtney did not have a hat. But, as H.M. took a Panama of regrettable design from the hat-rack, he followed the lumbering figure down the hall into a hot, silver, moonlight night.

Passers-by in the elm-shaded street might have been startled by a voice which marched beneath the elms. It was a strange, throaty, self-conscious voice, like that of a prophet in a trance or a ventriloquist talking bass.

"I will now," it suddenly announced, "give my readers some idea of the political situation as it existed between the years 1870 and 1880; and of the close attention with which I followed it even then."

Seven

"Over here," said Frank Sharpless, pointing. "Put her down on the bed."

Whatever he had thought he might be doing at ten-thirty that night, Courtney had not imagined that he would be carrying the body of an unconscious woman upstairs in a strange house, while the police muttered below.

But he was.

When he and H.M. arrived at the square white house, whose unfortunate name, "The Nest," was woven into the ironwork of the gate, they saw that the front door stood open and a light burned in the hall.

Sharpless, bearing in his arms a limp figure in a violet full-sleeved and full-skirted gown, stood in the hall arguing with an inspector of police from the Gloucestershire County Constabulary.

"She can't run away," Sharpless was insisting. "At least let me take her upstairs and make her comfortable."

The inspector hesitated.

"Very well, sir. But come down again straightaway; you understand?" He turned to the newcomers. "You'll be Sir Henry Merrivale, no doubt?" At H.M.'s nod he saluted. "Inspector Agnew here. Colonel Race told me to look out for you. Will you come this way, sir?"

The plan of the house was simple. It consisted of two long rooms on either side of the hall: front and back drawing room to the left, with a kitchen built out at the rear. Inspector Agnew's gesture indicated the library. From the back drawing room came a murmur of voices.

"I'm not," H.M. said sharply, "goin' to question anybody tonight. That can wait till tomorrow, when Masters gets here. But I'd like to hear a little more about it from you, son. Lead on."

"Phil," said Sharpless quickly, "stay here with me for a minute."

H.M., after giving assent to this with a nod and a sharp glance, followed Inspector Agnew into the library. Courtney was left with Sharpless and his charge. If Sharpless felt any surprise at seeing his friend there, he did not show it.

"Take Vicky," he ordered. "I'll lead the way."

She was attractive, Courtney thought. Damned attractive. Clumsily, and with some embarrassment, he carried her upstairs while Sharpless went ahead turning on lights.

The upper floor, built on a similar plan to the one below, consisted of six bedrooms and two bathrooms. Sharpless opened doors and tested lights until he found what was evidently Arthur and Vicky Fane's room—a spacious room at the front, on the right-hand side facing forward.

It was a pleasant bedroom, though its mixture of masculine and feminine tastes warred badly. A small white stone balcony over-looked the front lawn. The furniture was maplewood, the fitted carpet brown, the curtains old rose.

"Over here," said Sharpless. "Put her down on the bed."

He closed the door as Courtney did so, and they looked at each other.

"Frank," Courtney began, "in the name of—!"

"Sh-h!"

"Yes, but what's going on here? What did she do? If she's fainted, why not slosh some water on her and bring her round?"

Sharpless told him. A clock ticked on the table beside the bed; a bedside lamp, its shade of some pinkish glassy material over a mirror base, shed calm light on Vicky Fane's emotionless face; and a faint breeze stirred in the trees of the front lawn, moving the curtains. Sharpless neglected no detail of the story, while his companion stared.

"Look here, Frank, are you all mad?"

"No."

"You all swear none of you could have exchanged the real dagger for the rubber one?"

"That's right."

"And yet you also know nobody could have come in from outside to do it!"

"Also right. I proved it myself."

"Then," declared Courtney, "all I can say is you'd better begin to *un*prove it, and ruddy quick too."

"Oh? Why?"

"Man alive, listen! Get the fog out of your brain and think! Do you still love this girl?"

To answer this properly, it appeared, would require so many fervent words that Sharpless did not even try. He went over to the bed and pressed one of Vicky's hands.

"All right," said Courtney. "And she's yours now; had you realized it? Her husband's dead. That's motive. M-o-t-i-v-e, motive. If you prove that someone must have crept in from outside, that's fine. You're safe and clear. But if the police ever get the idea it must have been somebody in the room . . ."

Sharpless dropped Vicky's hand, and slowly turned round.

"So help me, Harry," he announced, driving his right fist into the palm of his other hand. "I never thought of it."

"Then you'd better begin to think of it."

"But why? Curse it all, they can't suspect me—or Rich or the Browning girl either, if it comes to that. We've got alibis like stone houses."

"You're sure of that?"

"Definitely."

"Well, just see you keep hammering it home to the police, that's all. Look here. Strictly between ourselves, *you* didn't. . . ?"

A curious smile traveled across Sharpless's face, having the equally curious effect of making him look older.

"No," he returned. "Besides, how did I do it? I'm no ghost or genius, whatever my superiors in the Royal Engineers may think." He consulted his wrist-watch. "Phil, I've got to get downstairs again, or the inspector will be kicking up a row. You stay here with her, will you?"

The hair rose on Courtney's conservative scalp.

"I can't stay here!"

"Oh, yes you can. And you're going to." Sharpless grew desperately serious. "Listen to me. You were very ha-ha this morning about my psychic fit. But there *was* something funny going on under the surface, and there still is. I can smell it. While I do, I'd just as soon Vicky wasn't out of the sight of somebody I can trust."

"Rubbish! You don't think anybody would try to—?"

"I was right once, and I can be right again. For the love of Mike don't make objections. It's not very much I'm asking you to do, is it? Just to stay here until I come up again? Then can't you be a decent bloke and oblige me for once?"

"All right, all right."

"Thanks. And now," said Sharpless, straightening the wings of his tie, "for more of the inquisition. I'll try not to be long. Make yourself at home."

The technique of making yourself at home under these conditions has not been defined by the best authorities.

Courtney, when the door had closed behind his companion, looked moodily round the room. He saw a brocaded chair, and rejected it. He tried to interest himself in the two or three pictures on the walls, but this floor also had its own creaks, and walking about produced them all as evidences of intrusion.

He could hear the ticking of the clock, and Vicky Fane's soft, steady breathing. She was attractive, right enough; but he thought he would be hanged if he let any woman land *him* in such a mess.

Between the windows stood a writing desk, scattered with Arthur Fane's possessions. A bank passbook lay neatly open, its pages held flat by a ruler. Courtney noted that Fane's current account at the Capital and Counties Bank contained the respectable total of twenty-two hundred pounds, and hastily averted his eyes. Wondering why anybody should keep so big a sum in a current account, when it might as well be out at interest, he stepped out through the full-length window on the balcony.

Two minutes later, the bedroom door softly opened.

Courtney, lost in the warm, grass-scented night, might not have heard this had it not been for the extreme furtiveness with which it was done—trying to avoid creaks and only succeeding in producing them.

He turned round.

A young woman with pale gold hair, and the sort of face favored by pre-Raphaelite painters, came in softly.

After a quick glance round the hall behind, she closed the door.

The mind of Philip Courtney, thirty-three and heart-whole, registered two things. First, that from the descriptions this must be Ann Browning, whom Sharpless had once designated as "wishy-washy" but whose employer described as "knowing a thing or two." Second, that she was the most desirable object Philip Courtney had seen in those same thirty-three years.

He stared, and stared again.

Her white gown, plain and cut low, emphasized both her fragility and her desirability. She glanced quickly round, making sure the room was empty. Circling round the bed, which had its head against the wall opposite the windows, she went to a dressing table placed cater-cornered in the left-hand angle of the same wall.

Courtney, tongue-tied but on the point of giving an explosive cough, remained where he was.

Over the dressing table was a large round looking-glass. The light of the bedside lamp touched it, dimly reflecting Ann's flushed cheeks and her absorbed, furtive eyes. Her body shielded what she was doing at the dressing table, which seemed to consist in searching among toilet articles there. Courtney heard glass rattle, and a sound as of fumbling among hairpins in a tray.

Then the door to the hall opened again.

"Oh!" said Ann, and straightened up.

The man who entered seemed as startled as she was.

He released his hand slowly from the knob, while the clock ticked. Again from the descriptions—a John Bullish man with funny hair—Courtney placed him as Dr. Richard Rich.

"I hope I don't intrude?" he inquired politely, in a soft bass voice.

"Oh, no!" smiled Ann. Courtney saw her profile reflected side-ways in the mirror, the lift of the chin and the slim rounded neck. "I thought I left my compact here, that's all. But it doesn't seem to be here."

"You know," smiled Rich, with the same meditative politeness, "I've often thought that a compact was the best excuse ever provided to womankind. We men have nothing so good." His tone changed. "Miss Browning, do you honestly doubt that Mrs. Fane is under hypnosis?"

"I don't understand what you mean?"

"Give me the pin, please," said Rich, extending his hand.

"Pin?"

"The pin you have in your hand."

While Ann raised her eyebrows, he walked over and took it gently from her fingers. A faint expression of relief flashed over her face as he turned away.

Rich bent over the woman on the bed. Unfastening two small catches at her wrist, he rolled back the sleeve of the gown almost to her shoulder. Courtney saw the long pin gleam as he turned it against the light.

"Watch!" instructed Rich.

Taking up Vicky's limp left arm, he held the flesh taut with his left hand. With his right he pressed the point of the pin against it. Then with his thumb he drove the pin full to its head in Vicky's arm.

It seemed to Courtney that Ann was about to utter a cry. A curious flavor of evil seemed to cling round this whole scene, though the source of it began in mist. Yet no word, or cry, or movement of any kind came from Vicky, who continued to breathe in sleep. Delicately, with deft fingers, Rich withdrew the pin so that no trace of blood showed.

"Two hundred years ago," he commented, "that would have hanged her as a witch. Thank heavens we're less superstitious. Or are we?" He turned round, smiling. "You'd better go downstairs, Miss Browning. I'm going to wake Mrs. Fane up. I don't relish the prospect, but..."

Ann walked over to the door.

"I really did come up here to get my compact," she assured him—and went out.

If it had not been for Dr. Rich's next movement, Courtney would have ended his own acute discomfort by stepping in from the balcony. But again he stopped. For Rich locked the door.

The sharp click of the key was like an omen. Rich, a red bar showing across his forehead, took one or two steps up and down the room. He seemed to be muttering to himself.

Then, drawing a deep breath, he went round the bed again to the dressing table side, where he bent over Vicky.

"Victoria Fane."

No change or stir.

"Victoria Fane." Whispering, the soft voice vibrated; it reached out into distances, and called beyond far doors.

"You hear me, Victoria Fane. You will not awake yet, but you hear me. Your mind is clear. You remember all the past, up to tonight. I wish to ask you something. You will answer me. You will speak nothing but the truth. Do you understand?"

The figure on the bed moaned.

Though a distinct sound, it was a mere whisper of the breath through her lips. Rich waited until the ticking of the clock seemed to have been lost in eternity.

"Victoria Fane, do you hate your husband?"

"Yes. No. Yes."

The eyes remained closed; the lips still barely moved; yet the struggle had returned.

"Why do you hate your husband?"

"Because he killed someone."

Rich remained motionless, bent over, his hand partly

supporting him on the tan quilted coverlet of the bed. His fingers closed into a fist.

"Whom did he kill?"

"A girl. Polly Allen. Here."

At mention of the name, Rich's bunched fingers tightened still more, and then relaxed.

"Here? In this room?"

"No. Downstairs.'

"Where downstairs? In the back drawing room, was it?"

"Yes!"

"How did he kill her?"

"He strangled her."

"Was it on the sofa he strangled her?"

"Yes!"

Again drawing a deep breath, Rich straightened up. He nodded to himself as though with enlightenment.

Courtney, it must be confessed, experienced something like a fit of the cold shivers. The commonplace well-to-do bedroom, like ten thousand other bedrooms in England, made a contrast for depths of violence: for ugly pictures under respectable paint.

"Is the song, *Drink to Me Only with Thine Eyes*," continued Rich, "is that song associated with what he did?"

"No!"

"What is it associated with, then?"

No reply.

"You must answer me. What is it associated with?"

"Frank Sharpless."

"Are you in love with Frank Sharpless?"

"Yes. Yes. Yes."

Rich put his small, stubby-fingered hands over his face, pressing in the eyes. Once more he nodded to himself. The brush of hair at the back of his head was agitated; it twisted and scuffed up over his collar.

"Does anyone else know about Polly Allen besides you?"

"Yes. Arthur's—"

Someone tried the knob of the door, and it was followed by a sharp knocking.

Rich, with a muttered exclamation, hurried round to the door and unlocked it. Outside stood Sir Henry Merrivale, Inspector Agnew, and Frank Sharpless. Rich's tone was composed and grave when he greeted them.

"Come in, gentlemen. I was just going to rouse Mrs. Fane. But perhaps it would be better to have a witness. Though I hardly think, Inspector, that that uniform of yours will help much."

Inspector Agnew regarded him suspiciously. "That's all right, sir. I'm not staying. Sir Henry'd like to have a word with you downstairs, if it's convenient. Oh, yes. And Captain Sharpless thinks *he* can—well, break the news to Mrs. Fane better than any of the rest of us."

Sharpless did not appear to like this.

"I didn't say that," he protested. "All I said was that it might come better from a friend than from a stranger." Pushing past the inspector and H.M., he entered the room. He stopped short beside the bed and peered round. "Hullo! Where's Phil Courtney got to?"

"Who, sir?"

"Phil Courtney. The fellow I left here not fifteen minutes ago."

Whereupon Courtney did what he felt he must do. It might be undignified, it might be unjustified, it might even be ludicrous. But before anybody had time to find him or even detect his presence, he put his hands on the rail of the balcony and vaulted softly over on to the lawn below.

Eight

Afterwards Courtney knew that he had done the right thing. It was the course reason prompted. But he was not, at that time, prompted by any cool reason.

He felt merely the blind instinct to get out of sight, so that he could have time to think, before he need face the implications of what he had just heard.

He landed in a flower-bed below, with little jar and almost without noise. But his conservative soul remained badly ruffled. To cap the events of the evening, he had now seen a girl who moved his pulses with uneasy effect, and he had gone sailing off a balcony with all the celerity of an escaping burglar or a detected Romeo.

Nobody saw him, for which he felt thankful. He walked up the front steps and entered the hall, with as much casualness as possible, through the open front door.

The hall was empty.

Well and just what *had* he learned? Assuredly it didn't tell against either Vicky Fane or Frank Sharpless. Arthur Fane, that solid man with the solid house, had strangled a girl named Polly Allen, and presumably disposed of her body. His wife knew it. But if she knew this, and wanted Fane out of the way so that she could marry Sharpless, she wouldn't have Sharpless kill Fane. She wouldn't need to. She and Sharpless would simply inform the police, and let the public hangman dispose of their obstacle.

He checked himself in these thoughts as H.M., Inspector Agnew, and Dr. Rich came down the stairs. The last-named was snappish in manner.

"Mrs. Fane's exhausted, I tell you," he was protesting. "She's weak; much weaker than I thought she would be. She hardly knows where she is. Do you think that young man's got enough tact to handle her?"

"Well, sir, she's awake now," Agnew pointed out. "And, anyway, Sir Henry'd like a word with you before he goes home."

"Curiously enough," replied Rich, slapping at the sleeves of his coat, "I should like a word with *him*."

He broke off as they all caught sight of Courtney.

"Ah," grunted H.M., peering over his spectacles; "and where have you been?"

"I strolled out to get a breath of fresh air. Mrs. Fane didn't seem to want much watching. She's all right now, I hope."

"No," said H.M. shortly. "She's bad. She's just about as bad as she can be, after these monkey-tricks. Never mind. What's this room here?"

He nodded towards a closed door at the back of the hall on the right-hand side as you faced the rear—just opposite the back drawing room.

"Dining room, sir," answered Agnew.

"Can we use it?"

"I don't see why not."

Agnew opened the door and switched on the lights—discovering nothing more than the spectacle of Uncle Hubert Fane standing at the sideboard, with a bottle tilted to his lips, improving the opportunity to steal a swig of his nephew's choicest liqueur brandy in the dark.

Hubert showed no embarrassment. He replaced the bottle, patted in the cork, wiped his mouth with a handkerchief, and, after giving them something between a nod and a formal bow, walked out of the room with such poise that nobody spoke a word to him.

"For the love of Esau," said H.M., pushing his spectacles back up so that he could look through them, "who was that?"

"Mr. Hubert Fane, sir. Mr. Fane's uncle."

"Uncle, eh?" said H.M. His eyes wandered to the notebook protruding from Courtney's pocket, and powerful emotions appeared to arise in him. "So that's his *uncle*, eh? Well, well, well! How very interestin'. I don't suppose *he's* ever been warned off the Turf, has he?"

Agnew jumped to attention.

"I don't know why you should say that, Sir Henry. But, just as it happens, the man who called to see Mr. Hubert Fane tonight was a bookmaker."

"You don't say?" observed H.M., musing with a darkly sinister expression which seemed to distend his whole face. But this clouded over. "No," he said. "No. There couldn't be *two* such crooks, not in the whole world. I got to let my reason govern me." He turned round. "You, sir, you're Dr. Rich?"

"I am."

"Sit down, will you?"

The dining room was of similar proportions to the back drawing room. A cluster of electric candles depended from the ceiling. The furniture, a genuine Jacobean set, showed rich and black in its carving against the cream-painted walls. Above the sideboard, over the silver and a bowl of fruit, hung one painting: a seventeenth-century child's head done on wood, whose fine tracing of cracks caught the light.

Rich drew out one of the tall chairs, and sat down.

"One moment," he said. He seemed to be bracing himself. He put his hands on his knees, and studied them. "Before you ask any questions, there's something I'd better tell you. I'd better tell you—" here he looked up—"that I have no longer any legal right to the title of doctor."

"So," said H.M. without inflection. "Why?"

"Because I was struck off the medical register eight years ago. You'll look all this up, of course."

"Struck off for doing what?"

Rich hesitated. He nodded towards Courtney and Inspector Agnew.

"Are these your colleagues?"

"Yes."

"Will what I say go no further . . . wait! unless it's necessary as evidence, of course?"

"Yes, sir," replied Agnew, "I think we can promise you that much, anyhow."

"I was accused," Rich went on, again without looking up, "of doing exactly what Captain Sharpless, in all innocence (I hope) mentioned last night. While practicing as a psychiatrist, I was accused of taking advantage of a lady when she was under hypnotic influence."

"So," said H.M. "Was the charge true?"

"The charge was *not* true," replied Rich, with suffused violence. His hands shook. "Every medical man runs similar dangers. He is a fool if he practices hypnotism without a witness present. Let me explain. Some dentists, for instance, refuse to give anesthetics to a female patient unless their assistants are present—as an assistant, but also as a witness." He lifted his eyes. "I'm speaking of medical matters. Do you understand me?"

"Yes, son. Very well."

Rich made a gesture.

"I was happily married, with two children. My wife took the children after the divorce."

He paused, and again made a gesture.

"I couldn't even understand the charge. Had it been

Hubert Fane, now, who was charged with that . . . but there we are. The thing meant ruin. Literal ruin."

"Is 'Richard Rich' really your name?"

"It is now. It wasn't then. It's the name I took when I went on the stage."

"On the stage?"

Rich lifted his shoulders.

"Well, a man must live. It was the only way I saw to make use of the profession I knew. Cheap, if you like; but legitimate. I was extremely adept at hypnotism. That was my act. What I did tonight I have done a thousand times. I never vary it; I seldom fail in it. That's how I happened to have that revolver with the carefully prepared dummy bullets."

"You did that turn on the stage?"

"No. Seldom on the stage. On the stage I used a usual, more hackneyed routine, sometimes with a girl-assistant named . . ." He waved his hand. "No matter. This was usually done at private parties in private houses: concerts, Christmas entertainments, and the rest of it. It isn't so well suited to a big hall. I agreed to perform tonight when Captain Sharpless clamored for it, because . . ."

"Because?"

Again Rich lifted his shoulders.

"Well, because I wanted another good dinner. Things have not been very easy, these days."

He brushed at his sleeve, and pushed back the shirt-cuff from his left wrist.

"So. Weren't you successful?"

"The idea," Rich replied candidly, "the routine, I thought was a good one. I still think so. I developed it myself. I thought it would take like wildfire. In fact, as far as interest is concerned, it can't fail. But—"

H.M. raised his eyebrows, prompting as Rich paused.

"But concert parties aren't so numerous. And I failed to take another danger into account. Once or twice—"

the shadow of a smile went over his face, despite the strained eyes and the mottled red color in his forehead—"once or twice, I regret to say, the good wife *has* pulled the trigger of the dummy gun. Result: uproarious delight, for the moment. But do you think the wife liked it? Or the husband liked it? Or that other people, when the word went round, wanted me to experiment on *them?* No. My trick had one great fault; it wasn't a trick. It worked."

Puffing out his breath, Rich looked down at his shirt-front, slapped the hands on his knees, and added abruptly:

"Successful? Do I look it?"

There was a silence.

H.M., scowling, turned round and lumbered to the windows at the end of the room. Outside, the rose-garden was silvered with moonlight. H.M. stared at it.

Philip Courtney could not help feeling a strong liking for the downcast, stocky little man in the chair. Everything Rich said had the ring of sincerity. You felt that he was, essentially, of a sincere and rather simple nature.

He had not mentioned certain facts which he had heard Vicky tell when she was under hypnosis. He had not passed on this information to the police—at least, not yet. But then neither had Courtney himself. And it was possible that Rich kept back this information out of ordinary decency.

H.M. swung round.

"As a matter of fact, d'ye see," H.M. told Rich, "what you've said really clears up the points I was goin' to ask about. I mean your credentials."

"I can produce what *were* my credentials. There was no fraud about my show, if that's what you mean."

"No," agreed H.M. "I don't think there was." The corners of his mouth drew down. "Who did you say insisted on your tryin' this 'experiment'?"

"Captain Sharpless."

"Yes; but who brought you to the house?"

"Hubert Fane."

"Oh? Did he suggest doin' it?"

"No. That was only incidental. To give Hubert his due: once he's seen thoroughly to his own comfort, he doesn't mind doing someone else a good turn. I used to know him years ago, when I was a reputable doctor. Then he went out to Kenya or somewhere, and I believe made money." Rich grimaced. "I wish to God *I* stood in his shoes."

H.M. ignored this.

"How long have you been givin' these concert parties of yours?"

"Oh, off and on for three or four years."

"Where?"

"All over the country."

"I see. And anybody who attended one of 'em would know what you'd use, what you'd do, and even how long it would take you to do it?"

"Yes, I suppose so."

"Humph. Yes. You see what we're gettin' at. Of these people here: do you remember ever havin' met any of 'em at any of your parties before tonight?"

Rich rubbed his head.

"My dear sir, that's almost impossible to say. It *is* impossible to say. Aside from Hubert, to the best of my knowledge I never set eyes on any of the people before last night. That's why—" his tone was whimsical—"I hope you won't suspect me of any complicity in Mr. Fane's death. I certainly didn't kill a man I'd never even met before. But as for any of them being present at one of my shows, all I can say is that I don't remember. At the same time . . ."

The door to the hall opened, and Ann Browning slipped in so unobtrusively that they might not even have noticed her had it not been for her white dress.

With a retiring but composed air, she took a chair behind Inspector Agnew, and sat down to listen.

H.M. stared at her.

"Oi!" he said, not gallantly. "Oi!"

"This is Miss Browning, Sir Henry, that I told you about," Agnew explained. "She's Colonel Race's private secretary. She's got the colonel's permission to be here, to report to him personally."

H.M.'s face grew apoplectic.

"Oh, she has, has she?"

"I do hope I'm not intruding," said Ann, in an anxious voice which would have mollified anyone. "And I won't bother you; really I won't. If you don't mind my just sitting and listening?"

"Besides, sir, since you've got your own private secretary with you," continued Agnew, nodding towards Courtney and the notebook in Courtney's pocket.

"I'm not—" snarled Courtney.

"Shut up," said H.M. austerely.

Courtney, about to correct this error, checked himself when he saw the look Ann Browning directed towards him. It was one of quickening, friendly interest: an opening of the eyes and a half-smile of the lips: and it sent warmth through him.

"Now then," glowered H.M., putting his fists on his hips and staring everybody down, "if these interruptions will stop puttin' me off for a minute or two, I'll end this as quick as I can." He looked at Rich. "You said you couldn't remember whether you'd seen any of 'em before. Then you said, 'At the same time—' At the same time, what?"

Rich frowned. "I'm glad Miss Browning is here. Because I've got a half impression, if I can call it that, of having seen her somewhere before. Or was it Mrs. Fane herself? I cannot be sure."

"Seen her where?"

"I don't know."

82

"At one of your entertainments?"

"That, on my honor, I can't say."

H.M. turned to Ann. "You ever seen that feller before?" he inquired, pointing a big flipper.

Ann looked puzzled. "No, I'm almost sure I haven't," she smiled. "And I'm sure I should have remembered Dr. Rich."

"Miss Browning, at least, isn't of a very trusting nature," observed Rich, with an expression which removed offense. "I think she was inclined to doubt whether Mrs. Fane was really under hypnosis. A little while ago, she was going to apply the elementary test of sticking a pin into the victim to find out. So I applied the pin."

He related the incident just as it had taken place. But he added nothing else.

"Dr. Rich, I don't think that's very nice of you!" said Ann, appealing to the others. "I really wasn't going to do anything of the sort. But it's just as well we know, isn't it?"

H.M. peered round the group.

"Now look here," he said. "I'm not goin' to ask for your individual stories, any of you. There's a chap coming from London tomorrow who'll do that. I'll just say this. Is there *anything* else, anything you can tell me, except what you've already told the inspector here? Did anything else happen except what you've mentioned?"

"No," answered Rich firmly.

"Nothing," agreed Ann.

H.M. heaved a gusty sigh.

"All right, then. Cut along home. I'm goin' home myself to do a little sittin' and thinkin' while I dictate."

Five minutes later, the front door closed behind Courtney and H.M. The latter turned down the brim of his Panama hat all round. His companion thought he was going to start towards the gate. Instead he heard the rattle of a match box, and saw a small flame spring up.

H.M. lumbered to the side of the lawn. Holding up the match, he bent down to inspect a flower-bed under the first-floor balcony. The tiny flame showed two large footprints stamped into the soil.

H.M. turned, the match-flame glinting evilly on his spectacles.

"Uh-huh," he said. "I thought so. I thought I saw you duck. Now are you goin' to tell me what really happened up in that bedroom; or is even my biographer mixed up in this funny business?"

Up over their heads, a shadow stirred in the moonlight.

They did not see it.

Nine

At three o'clock on the following afternoon, Chief Inspector Humphrey Masters unlatched the gate of Major Adams's house in Fitzherbert Avenue.

It was a blistering day, Thursday the twenty-fourth of August. Yet Masters, though he always feels the heat, was buttoned up in blue serge and wore his usual bowler hat. Just inside the gate he stopped short.

For an idyllic scene was in progress on the front lawn.

Sir Henry Merrivale, in a white short-sleeved shirt and white flannels, was engaged in playing clock-golf. Near him in a wicker chair sat a solid-looking young man of thirty-odd, smoking a pipe and making shorthand notes. Another chair was occupied by a fair-haired girl in a print frock, who had both hands pressed to her face as though to keep from exploding.

Thus far, pastoral ease merged into drowsiness. The lawn was of that smooth, shimmering green which seems to have lighter stripes in it. Against it shone the white clock-numerals and the little red metal flag which marked the cup. A low, gabled house, elm-shaded, rose against the green-blue haze of the Cotswolds beyond.

H.M.'s style with the putter was correct. Even his shirt and flannels were reasonably correct. But on his head he wore an encumbrance which made even Masters recoils. It was a broad-brimmed, high-crowned conical hat of loose-woven straw, of the sort that darkies in the Southern states of America are accustomed to put on their horses.

Then, too, there was the voice.

"I will now deal," said this voice, "with my first term away at school, and the many happy memories it brings back to me. I will tell how Digby Dukes and I changed round the organ-pipes in the chapel at St. Just's one Saturday night in the autumn of '81.

"This rearrangement was done with skill and care. No pipe was placed very far away from its original position, so that the rearrangement could not be detected by a casual glance. But the general effect, when the organist crashed into the opening bars of the first hymn on Sunday morning, had to be heard to be believed.

"Even then all might have been well if the organist, old Pop Grossbauer, had not lost his head and attempted to play the hymn through. The resultin' sounds, until the headmaster went up and dragged Pop gibberin' away from the organ, will be remembered at St. Just's as long as iron is strong or stone abides. I can liken it only to an interview between Adolf Hitler and Benito Mussolini when each is under the impression that the other has stolen his watch."

The fair-haired girl pressed her hands still harder over her face, and began to rock back and forth.

The pipe-smoking young man preserved the gravity of a Spanish grandee as he continued to make notes.

" 'Stolen his watch . . .'?" he prompted, as H.M. paused. "Yes?"

H.M. pondered deeply before resuming.

And Chief Inspector Masters walked up the lawn, removing his hat.

"Ah, sir!" he said.

"So it's you," said H.M., breaking off and squinting round evilly over the putter.

"Yes, sir, it's me. And," said Masters grimly, "you don't need to tell me. I know. We're in it again. Another impossible situation. And you deliberately had me sent for."

"You sit down and be quiet," said H.M. sternly. "I've got another chapter to dictate before I can talk to you. Making. . . ?"

He looked round inquiringly at the note-taker.

"About twenty-eight thousand words since breakfast-time," replied Courtney, taking the pipe out of his mouth. "Not counting the ten thousand last night."

"You hear, Masters?"

"But may I ask, sir, what in lum's name you're *doing*?"

"I'm dictatin' my reminiscences."

"Your what?"

"My me-moirs," said H.M. accenting his version of the first syllable. "My autobiography."

Masters stood very still. Bland as a card-sharper, with his grizzled hair carefully brushed to hide the bald-spot, he stood in the strong sunshine like a man struck by certain apprehensions.

"Oh, ah? What you'd call your life story, eh?"

"That's it. Shrewd lad, Masters."

"I see. You—er—you haven't said anything about *me* in it, have you?"

"No, not yet," admitted H.M. He chortled. "But, oh, my eye, is it goin' to be juicy when I do!"

"I warn you, sir—!"

The young man interposed smoothly. "If I were you, Chief Inspector," he suggested, "I shouldn't trouble. We've done roughly forty-eight thousand words, and he's just into his eleventh year. If he's got anything against you, I should begin to worry about it round about next Christmas."

H.M. pointed with a putter.

"I got a suspicion," he said, "a very strong suspicion, that that blighter there is always on the edge of making smart cracks at me. But he's got a cast-iron face. I'm serious about this book. It's goin' to be an important social and political document. You." He leered round at Ann Browning. "Were *you* laughin' at me?"

The girl took her hands away from her face.

"You know I wouldn't do that," she assured him, with such apparent sincerity that he subsided. "But Mr. Courtney's fingers must be numb by this time. Why don't you take a breather so that the chief inspector can tell you what he's come to tell you?"

Masters stiffened.

"Morning, miss," he said noncommittally, but with a significant glance at H.M. He looked at Courtney. "Morning, sir."

H.M. performed introductions.

"This gal," he added, "is Race's protegée. She's been given instructions to stick to me, so there's nothing you can do about it, son."

Masters regarded Ann with a quickening of interest.

"And is also (eh?) the young lady who was present at that business last night? Glad to hear it, miss! You're the only person concerned I haven't had a word with yet."

H.M. blinked.

"So? That's quick work, ain't it, Masters?"

"Four o'clock in the afternoon, sir. *If* you don't mind my pointing it out."

"Now, now. Less of the heavy copper stuff, son. What have you been up to?"

Masters inhaled a mighty breath.

"I've talked to Agnew, and read through his notes. I've had a word with Mrs. Fane, Captain Sharpless, Mr. Hubert Fane, Dr. Rich, the maid, and the cook. I've been carefully over that sitting room where the murder was done."

"And?"

"You," suggested Masters pointedly, "tell me."

H.M. cast down the putter. He went to the porch and returned carrying two beach-chairs. These, after a struggle vaguely suggesting Laocoon, in which the chairs folded into shapes even more incomprehensible than is their usual custom, he managed to set straight for Masters and himself.

"It's like this," the chief inspector continued, putting his hat down on the grass. "If only these people wouldn't be so ruddy pat with their stories! If only they wouldn't *all* swear they saw each other *all* the time! If only—" He stopped, remembering that he was speaking in front of one of them.

"It's perfectly true, though," Ann assured him.

Masters craned round. His tone grew confidential.

"Come, now, miss! Just among ourselves. How can you be so sure of that?"

"Because four of us then were sitting as close together as the four of us are here now. With Dr. Rich in the middle, like this."

Ann reached out after the putter, and stood it up in the middle to represent Rich.

"The bridge lamp was shining down directly on us. The table was at least twelve feet away—"

"Just twelve feet," said Masters. "I measured it."

"And the circle wasn't broken," concluded Ann. "The only one who ever went near the table was Arthur Fane himself."

"I say, Masters," interposed H.M., who was leaning back in the beach-chair and had his revolting hat tilted over his spectacles. "What's your notion of the suggestion that somebody sneaked in by way of the door or the windows?"

Masters hesitated.

"Go on, son! Speak up."

"Well, sir, I say I'm smacking well certain nobody did. It's not just that I take the word of the people in the room, though I can see what they tell me is reasonable enough. But—as regards the door—I've got an independent witness."

"A witness? Who?"

"Daisy Fenton, the maid."

Masters took out his notebook.

"Now, this girl Daisy had been curious, real hot-and-bothered curious, about what was being done that night. She knew there was some hypnotism game going on, but she didn't know what. Any girl would be curious, I expect. So, from the time that crowd went into the back sitting room after dinner to the time Mr. Fane was stabbed, Daisy never left the front hall."

"Wow!" said H.M.

Masters nodded grimly. "Just so, sir."

"But—"

"Stop a bit, now. Daisy hung about the hall. A little later, she saw Mrs. Fane come out of the sitting room for that part where Mrs. Fane was asked to go out, like a guessing game.

"Daisy shied back into the dining-room door, where it was dark, and waited. She says Mrs. Fane listened at the door, which wasn't quite caught, until somebody closed it from inside. Then after a few minutes Dr. Rich opened it, and invited Mrs. Fane back in. All just as we've heard.

"Back went Daisy to her post in the hall. A little while after this, the front doorbell rang. It was a bookie named MacDonald, asking to see Mr. Hubert Fane. Daisy tried to send him away, but he wasn't having any. So down she went to the sitting room, and fetched out Mr. Hubert Fane."

Masters paused, clearing his throat.

The late afternoon sun blazed on his forehead. To

Courtney, the scene last night unfolded in vivid colors, even though he had not seen it.

"Mr. Hubert Fane came out, and spoke to the bookie on the front steps. They were arguing about something—Daisy could see 'em all the time—while Daisy remained where she was, in the hall, with one ear on the door."

H.M., who had been breathing as though in sleep under the hat, here opened one eye.

"Hold on, son! Wasn't she afraid old Hubert might get shirty if he saw her hangin' about obviously listening at door?"

Masters shook his head.

"No. She says she knew he wouldn't say anything to her. She says he never does. She says—" Masters' tone took on a note of heavy mimicry—"she says he's 'such a dear old gentleman.' "

"Uh-huh. Go on."

"Mr. Hubert Fane finished his talk with the bookie, and came back into the hall. He walked into the dining room, took a nip of brandy off the sideboard (as I'm told his habit is), walked straight back again to the sitting-room door, and opened it just about ten seconds after Mr. Arthur Fane was stabbed. In other words, he's got every bit as good an alibi as anybody in that room."

Masters shut up his notebook with a slap.

"But the important thing (eh?) is Daisy's testimony. She swears—and so help me, sir, I don't see any reason to doubt her—that nobody could have sneaked past her while she was there. And that's our witness. It washes out the door."

"Yes. I was afraid of that."

"Do you agree, Sir Henry, or don't you?"

H.M. groaned.

"All right, son. I agree. What about the windows?"

"I gave those windows a good going-over. Under

them there's a four-foot-wide flower-bed that was watered down late in the afternoon, and would show traces if you as much as breathed on it. The windows are eight feet up. They've got an unbroken coating of dust across the sills; thick dust. You know what the floor inside is like. The table was twelve feet from the windows. The curtains were drawn, and our witnesses swear they never moved. Lummy! Aside from having the windows locked and bolted on the inside, which they'd hardly be on an August night, I don't see how it could be more impossible for anybody to have got in. It washes out the windows as well."

"Yes," admitted H.M., "it does."

Philip Courtney found his wits whirling.

He had hoped that the night would bring good counsel, or at least some flaw in the evidence. But now the room seemed sealed up, as though with gummed paper, worse than ever.

"But the thing's impossible!" he said.

Masters turned slowly round and contemplated him. He had the air of a man who, though lost in a strange land, yet hears an old familiar tune.

"Ah," murmured the chief inspector. "Now where have I heard that before? Lummy, where have I heard it before? But look at Sir Henry there! It doesn't seem to bother *him* any."

H.M. had, indeed, a singularly peaceful air as he lay back in the chair. A fly circled round and settled down on the peak of his hat.

"The case," pursued Masters, "has got to be approached in a different way. It's all crazy and back-to-foremost to start with. We begin by knowing the murderer; but the murderer's the only person who can't be guilty. We—"

"Now, now, son!" urged H.M. soothingly.

But Masters was getting steam up.

"We've got to find someone who exchanged a real

dagger for a rubber one, when the evidence proves nobody could have done it. It's no good saying, 'Where were you at such-and-such a time?' We know where they were. It's no good saying, 'How do you explain this bit of suspicious behavior?' Because there isn't any suspicious behavior. There's no behavior at all. Hypnotism! Rubber daggers! Urr!"

He drew his sleeve across his forehead.

"Now, Masters, you're gettin' yourself all hot . . . !"

"Yes, sir, I am; and I admit it. Who wouldn't be? If you can suggest any explanation of how those daggers could have been exchanged, I'd be glad to hear it. But, so far as I can see, there isn't any."

"Oh, my son! Of course there's an explanation!"

"An explanation that fits all the facts?"

"An explanation that fits all the facts."

"And you know it?"

"Sure. It's easy."

Masters got up from his chair, but sat down again. H.M. struggled up to a sitting position.

"No, son: I'm not just actin' the cryptic. I really am worried. I'm afraid that if I tell you this explanation you'll go harin' off on the wrong track."

"I can believe evidence, Sir Henry."

"Yes. I know. That's what worries me. See here." H.M. ruffled the tips of his fingers across his forehead. "For the sake of argument, do you believe the stories of these witnesses—Ann Browning, Captain Sharpless, Dr. Rich, Hubert Fane—that none of 'em went near the table at any time?"

"What else can I do? Unless the whole thing's a quadruple-put-up job, with everybody lying, what else can I do? I'm bound to accept it."

"All right. Do you also believe that nobody could have got in from outside?"

"Ah! That I do, and I don't mind admitting it."

H.M. looked distressed.

"So. Then, according to the evidence, there's only one explanation that *can* be true. It's been an odd blind spot that nobody seems to have noticed before."

"If you mean," retorted Masters, regarding him with broad and fishy skepticism, "that Mr. Arthur Fane exchanged the daggers himself . . . well, I'll just say ha-ha and let it go at that. Mr. Fane knew he was going to be stabbed with that dagger. He insisted on it. He had a spot drawn over his heart so it couldn't be missed. Don't tell me any man plans suicide in quite that way. But Mr. Fane was the only person who did go near that table."

H.M. sighed.

"Got it," he said.

"Got what?"

"The blind spot. Burn me, we've been repeatin' the story about nobody goin' near the table so often that it's stopped having any meaning.

"We're forgetting that there was somebody who admittedly did go near the table. Not only near it; but to it, in plain sight. Somebody who stood with her back to the witnesses so that her body shielded the table in a darkish part of the room. Somebody who wore a full-sleeved dress tight at the wrists. Somebody who could, therefore, have slipped the real dagger out of her sleeve, and the rubber dagger back in its place, as quick as winking."

H.M. looked still more glum and angry.

"In short," he concluded, "Mrs. Fane herself."

Ten

Ann sat very still, her breath coming slowly. Her heels were together, her eyes on the ground. When she raised her head to look at H.M., so that the sun flashed gold on her hair, her eyes were brilliant but incredulous.

"Oh, that's absurd!" Ann protested. "You mean she wasn't really hypnotized at all? And only pretended to be? Impossible! Besides, I know Vicky well and I'm awfully fond of her. She'd never—"

"So? Aren't you the gal," queried H.M., peering over his spectacles, "who went up to her bedroom especially to stick her with a pin and find out?"

Ann clenched her hands.

"I went up there to get my compact. I really did, though nobody will believe me!"

Masters' face wore a far-off, satisfied smile for the first time that day.

"Well, well, well!" mused the chief inspector, and rubbed his hands. "Now this is something like evidence, I don't mind telling you!"

H.M. uttered a groan.

"Just confidentially," pursued Masters, cheering up, "I never did like all this hypnotic funny business, and that's a fact. Oh, I know it's scientifically true, all right!

We bumped into it in that Mantling case years ago.* But here—no, it didn't just look right to me, somehow. Hold on, though. Stop a bit." He frowned, fingering his jaw. "That pin business. Mrs. Fane was stuck with a pin, wasn't she? And she didn't even so much as blink?"

"She was," agreed Ann firmly. "I saw it done."

"Uh-huh," said H.M. "So did somebody else." He turned to Masters. "Do you happen to have a pin on you, son?"

"What for?"

"Never mind what for. If you got a pin," said H.M., opening and shutting his hand, "gimme."

After staring at him for a moment, Masters turned back the lapel of his jacket, revealing two pins stuck through the underside.

" 'See a pin and pick it up, and all the day you'll have good luck,' " he quoted, not without jocularity. "My old mother taught me that years ago, and I've never been able to resist—"

"Stow the gab," said H.M., "and gimme."

Masters handed it over.

Holding the pin in his mouth, H.M. reached into his pocket and took out a box of matches. Squinting, he held the pin by the head in his left hand, and carefully moved the match-flame over it from end to end.

"I hope our friend Rich," he grunted, "sterilized that pin before he used it on Mrs. Fane?"

"He didn't, that I remember," said Ann.

"So? Careless. And blinkin' dangerous too. Now watch closely, and the old man'll give you a demonstration."

Holding his left forearm against his leg so that the skin was taut, H.M. searched for a place in the upper

---

*See *The Red Widow Murders*, William Morrow and Company, 1935.

side of the forearm. He set the point of the pin there, and with a quick push drove it to the head in his arm.

Everyone had instinctively stiffened in protest. It formed a grotesque contrast: the late afternoon sunshine, the quiet green lawn with the white clock-golf numerals, and the push that drove steel into flesh.

"Brr!" said Ann, moving her shoulders. "But *you* didn't jump?"

"No, my wench. Because it didn't hurt, I didn't even feel it."

Masters regarded him incredulously.

"True, son," H.M. assured him. "Just a medical fact, like hypnotism. This is an old parlor trick, well known to conjurors and—"

He paused, blinking. Then his eyes grew fixed as he looked into vacancy, and a sniff rumbled through his nose. An idea seemed to be stirring with considerable effect. In the same dream he stretched out his right hand, moving the fingers as though pressing something. But, as the others clamored at him, he woke up.

"No!" he snapped. "Burn it all, I'm no Yogi. Anybody can do this. You can do it yourselves, if you choose a part of the arm where you don't hit a vein or an artery, make sure the skin is firm, and drive it in firmly." He plucked out the pin, which was followed by not a speck of blood. "Like to try it?"

"No, thanks," shivered Ann.

"Let me have a go," requested Courtney.

He was not at all easy about this. But Ann's eyes were on him, and he tried not to hesitate. Baring his left arm to the elbow, he took the pin (which H.M. insisted on sterilizing again), set it to his arm, gritted his teeth, and . . .

"Ow!" he yelled, bouncing as though an adder had bitten him.

Nor was he soothed by H.M.'s manifest glee.

"I knew I was goin' to crack your poker-face sooner

or later," declared H.M. Then his tone changed. "You didn't work it," he explained patiently, "because you were instinctively afraid of hurtin' yourself. You jabbed it in with a little bit of a push to see if you would feel it, and so of course you did. That's not the way, son. Your subconscious—"

"Everything in this ruddy case," said Masters, "is subconscious. Look here, sir: this trick really works?"

"Oh, son, of course it does. You saw me do it. Wants practice and strength of mind, naturally."

Masters eyed him.

"You're full of tricks, aren't you?"

"He is," said Courtney, plucking the pin from a smarting arm. "If you were taking down his memoirs, Chief Inspector, you'd realize that that's all he ever thinks about."

H.M. looked pleased.

"I've got a theory," Courtney pursued, "that it's the explanation of how he catches murderers. His mind works like theirs."

"But the point is," insisted Masters, sweeping this aside, "that this thing is practical and Mrs. Fane *could* have been shamming. Hold on, though! It was Dr. Rich who worked that game. Does that mean he was in cahoots with her?"

"No, no, no, no, no!" growled H.M. "It doesn't mean Mrs. Fane was shamming, and it doesn't mean Rich was in cahoots with her. Rich knew very well she wasn't shamming—"

"Oh?" inquired Masters skeptically.

"—or he wouldn't have asked her certain questions later, under hypnosis, that I'm goin' to tell you about in a minute. But this gal here—" he pointed at Ann— "was doubtful. So Rich took the opportunity of getting rid of her quickly by a trick. That's all."

Masters took out his notebook. He balanced it on his

knee. He shot back his shirt-cuffs, to make plain that his words would be careful and weighty.

"Now listen to me for a minute, sir. You yourself admit that Mrs. Fane is the only person who *could* be guilty. Now don't you?"

"According to the evidence, yes."

"Just so. And she could have shammed being hypnotized, couldn't she?"

"I s'pose so."

"In a way that could have deceived even Dr. Rich himself? Just so!" Masters was warming up again. "It'd take a thundering good piece of acting, granted. But we've met these good actresses before. Remember Glenda Darworth? And Janet Derwent? And Hilary Keen?

"She could have switched the daggers, right enough. The next question is: what happened to the rubber dagger afterwards? She 'slipped it in her sleeve,' you suggest. But it didn't stay there. Where is the rubber dagger, then? Agnew tells me he made a thorough search of that back sitting room, but he didn't find it."

"No," said H.M. disconsolately. "*I* found it."

"You found it?"

H.M. reached into his trousers pocket. He took out the rubber dagger, flimsy and tawdry-looking against sunlight, its scratched silver paint showing shreds and patches of darker rubber beneath. He bent it back and forth.

"Where did you find that thing, sir?"

"In the sofa. Poked down between the bottom and back cushions, out of sight. On the same sofa where Mrs. Fane was lyin' afterwards, presumably hypnotized."

The ensuing pause, as they all envisaged Vicky Fane lying there, was not more sinister than Masters' rather affable voice.

"You don't tell me now?" inquired the chief inspector, taking the dagger from H.M. and examining it. "And when did you find it there?"

"Last night."

"Last night? Then why in blazes couldn't you have said something about it?"

H.M. scratched the side of his nose.

"For the same reason I'm not awful keen on showing it now. Masters, the idea is a beauty. I admit that. Woman gets herself (apparently) hypnotized. Then polishes off her husband. And everybody thinks, as you say, that the murderer is the only person who can't possibly be guilty."

"The idea," breathed Ann, "is horrid and fascinating at the same time. It would be rather awful, wouldn't it, if somebody we thought figured in one rôle really figured in exactly the opposite rôle?"

Though H.M. showed a passing gleam of interest in this, turning round to look at her, he addressed Masters again.

"All the evidence shouts belief. Oh, my eye, doesn't it? The plot is perfect. The motive is there. The evidence is strong. There's only just one little difficulty about it."

"What's that?"

"It ain't true," said H.M.

Masters was commencing to lose his temper.

"What's the good of saying that, sir? When you yourself will admit—"

"This feller," interrupted H.M., pointing at Courtney, "was out on the balcony of Mrs. Fane's bedroom between the time Frank Sharpless carried her up there almost to the time she was waked up out of her sleep. Now listen to what he has to say; and then go and eat worms."

Phil Courtney was hotly uncomfortable. Ann's eyes flashed round to his, startled: he avoided them, but he retained the memory of them while he told his story.

He remembered how H.M. had dragged the facts out of him last night, standing in the moonlight in front of Fane's house, with the shadows of the elms against the sky. It sounded, he thought (or at least it must sound to Ann) like the tale of a prowler and a spy. Yet for Vicky Fane's sake he was glad to tell it, and very quick to tell it.

Masters stared at him.

"There's no joke about this, sir?" the chief inspector demanded.

"No. I can swear to every word of it."

Masters was incredulous. "Mr. Fane, *that* respectable chap, killed this girl Polly Allen because—hurrum?"

"It's been done before, y'know," H.M. pointed out. "In fact, you and I can both remember a few names in that way. If you're quotin' cases to me, do you remember who used the atropine in the Haye business?"*

"Just a minute, sir!" urged Masters. "But what did he do with the girl afterwards, Mr. Courtney? There's no murder ever been reported. At least, as far as Agnew mentioned to me."

Courtney could not help him.

"All I can tell you," he replied, "is Mrs. Fane's answers to Rich's questions."

"Under hypnosis? Or at least so *she* pretended?"

"If you insist on that, yes. Arthur Fane strangled this girl on the sofa in the back drawing room. That's as far as Rich got with his questioning before he was interrupted. He had just asked, 'Does anybody else know about this?' and she said, 'Yes,' and was going to tell him who, when they knocked at the door and he had to stop."

"Mrs. Fane didn't say who else knew about it?"

"No."

---

*See *Death in Five Boxes*, William Morrow & Company, 1938.

"Now think it over," interposed H.M., himself making a mesmeric pass. "Our good Fane, who was undoubtedly rather a lad as a skirt-chaser—"

(Here, Courtney noticed, Ann shivered.)

"Our good Fane has committed a crime for which the punishment is fairly well known. His wife knows it. All right. Suppose she hates it. Suppose she hates him like hell. Suppose she wants another man. Is she deliberately goin' to kill him like that, when all she's got to do is tip off the police?"

Silence.

And checkmate.

Westwards over Cheltenham, the low-lying sun made a dazzle among white and red roofs. It also lighted the broad and fishily skeptical expression on Masters' face.

"All very well," he conceded. "*If* it's true. *If* Mrs. Fane didn't make up the story herself."

"Well, son, it ought to be easy enough to prove. That's your job. Go to Agnew. Trace Polly Allen. Find out. But if it does turn out to be true, as I'm bettin' it will—Masters, you've got no more case against Mrs. Fane than Paddy's goat."

Masters jumped to his feet.

"Look out!" howled H.M. "You'll step on your hat!"

Masters seemed to meditate giving the hat a swift kick. Instead, with powerful dignity, he corked himself; but the ruddiness of his countenance was not caused by the heat.

H.M. turned to Ann.

"What do you say?" he asked softly. "You knew Fane pretty well. Would you say he was capable of an act like that?"

Ann looked away from him, down at the grass. Again Courtney saw the clear profile: the mouth wide and full-lipped, the nose a little broad for complete beauty. He had an impression that she wanted to tell them something, and was almost on the point of telling it, yet checked herself.

"I didn't know him well," she defended herself, scuffing the toe of her shoe in the grass.

"Who is, or was, this Polly Allen? Did you know her?"

Ann shook her head emphatically.

"I've never even heard the name. She was probably—well!"

"But you haven't answered my question. Would you say Arthur Fane might do a thing like that?"

She faced him.

"Yes, I think he might. Judging from what I know of his family. And certain things." She hesitated. Her eyes revealed themselves as penetrating and intelligent. "But when was this girl killed?" Her voice quickened. "Was it about the middle of July? The fourteenth or the fifteenth?"

"I can't say," returned Courtney. "Mrs. Fane didn't say anything about that."

"Wait!" snapped H.M. "Why that date?"

"Because I went to the house that night," answered Ann.

There was a stir in the group. Even Masters whirled round from looking at the clock-golf outfit.

"It probably doesn't mean anything! Please! I only—"

"All the same," said H.M., "what about it?"

She moistened her lips.

"Nothing. I went over to Vicky's to see whether I could borrow some wool. I live only a stone's throw away from here anyway. It was well past ten o'clock, but in those days the light held until nearly ten. It was the fourteenth . . . no, the fifteenth of July! I remember, because some French friends of mine gave a party the day before; and that was Bastille Day, the fourteenth."

"Yes?"

"I rang the front doorbell, but there was no answer and I couldn't see any lights in the house. I didn't think they could all be away—even servants. But I rang again, and still there was no answer. I was just going away when Arthur opened the door."

"Go on."

"He was in his shirt-sleeves. That's how I remember. It was the first time I'd ever seen him in his shirt-sleeves. He just said Vicky wasn't at home, and closed the door in my face. Rather rudely, I thought. I went away."

The account was unadorned and even commonplace, but her listeners found it anything but commonplace.

Courtney felt again the sense of evil, whose origin he could not trace, but which had touched him the night before. Ann's story conjured up visions of unexpected things behind starched window-curtains: of a dark house, and something lying on a sofa. It is not always wise to explore too far the possibilities of a summer night.

"And that's all you know?"

"That's everything, I swear!"

Masters was uneasy. "And not very much either, miss, if you don't mind my saying so. However, we'll go into this! I can promise you that. But—"

"But what, son?" asked H.M. quietly.

"*Somebody* killed Mr. Fane! First you show me a great big beautiful case against Mrs. Fane. Then you try to tear it down by saying she hadn't got a motive, just because she hated her husband so much. What's up your sleeve, sir? Because I'm smacking well certain there is something."

H.M. twiddled his thumbs.

"Well . . . now. I wouldn't go so far as to say that. But I do think, Masters, you may not be payin' enough attention to motive. That's what bothers me like blazes: motive."

"I'll argue it with pleasure," returned Masters, whipping out his notebook again with the air of a duelist, "if you think it'll get us anywhere. Which it won't. Let's look at the list of people, and see what we have.

"First, Mrs. Fane herself. We've talked about that.

"Second, Captain Sharpless. H'm. Might have had a motive. It strikes me he's pretty far gone on Mrs. Fane, *that* young gentleman. But he can't have done it, because every witness is willing to swear he couldn't have changed the daggers.

"Third, Mr. Hubert Fane. No motive that I can see. He's a wealthy old gent, they tell me; and even if he wasn't, he doesn't inherit a penny under Arthur Fane's will. (Mr. Fane's money, by the way, is all left to his wife, and to charity if she dies; think that over about her ladyship.) Finally, Mr. Hubert Fane's got as good an alibi as anybody else.

"Fourth, Dr. Rich. No motive whatever. Not a ghost of one. And the same applies to him as to Captain Sharpless: he couldn't have done it.

"Fifth and last, Miss Browning."

Masters broke off, with his deceptive air of heartiness, and grinned at Ann.

"I hope you don't mind being included, miss?"

"No, no, of course not!"

"No motive," said Masters. "At least, none we've heard." He winked at her apologetically. "And the same thing for the practical side: she couldn't have changed the daggers."

Masters shut up his notebook and shook it in the air.

"Now, sir! That's the lot. Unless you want to drag in Daisy Fenton, the maid, or Mrs. Propper, the cook—"

"I say, Masters." Again H.M. ruffled his fingers across his forehead. "This cook, now. You got a statement from the maid. Could the cook add anything to it?"

"Mrs. Propper? No. She always goes to bed at nine sharp on the top floor of the house. She didn't even hear the rumpus last night.

"But as I say, that's the lot. That's a list of both motive and opportunity. Will you just tell me where in lum's name you can find either a motive *or* an opportunity?"

Courtney, who was facing Major Adams's house, saw khaki and gilt buttons swing round the side of it. Frank Sharpless, the declining sun picking out the expression of his eyes even at that distance, hurried across towards them.

There was, Courtney remembered, a grassy elm-shaded lane or alley which ran at the back of all these houses parallel with the street in front. Sharpless had evidently taken a short cut from the Fanes' house. Courtney thought with uneasiness that it was damned indiscreet of him to go there today. Gossip would be wagging a long enough tongue already.

But this idea was swept away as Sharpless approached.

"Sir Henry," he began without preliminary, "you said last night you remembered me. Anyway, you know my father. Colonel Sharpless?"

"Yes, son?"

"Is it true that you've got a medical degree as well as a legal one?"

"Yes. That's right."

"Then," said Sharpless, running a finger round inside his khaki shirt-collar, "will you for God's sake come down and have a look at Vicky? Now?"

The summer evening was very still.

"What's wrong with her?"

"I don't know. I've phoned for her own doctor, but he lives at the other side of town. And she's worrying me more every minute. First she complained of stiffness in the back of the neck. Then a funny feeling in her jaws, painful. Then—she wouldn't let me send for a doctor; but I insisted—then—"

All expression was smoothed out of H.M.'s face. He adjusted his spectacles, and looked steadily through them. Yet Courtney caught the wave of emotion in the air, as palpably as the body gives out heat; and that emotion was fear.

H.M.'s tone was wooden. "How long has this been goin' on, son?"

"About an hour."

"Lookin' a bit seedy all day, has she?"

"Yes, she has."

"So. Any difficulty in swallowing?"

Sharpless thought back. "Yes! I remember, she complained about it at tea, and wouldn't drink much."

Sharpless's quick intuition caught the atmosphere about him. H.M.'s eyes moved briefly, too briefly, towards Courtney's hands. Courtney was still holding, and absent-mindedly bending, the pin he had tried to thrust painlessly into his arm.

Then H.M. took out his watch, consulted it, and moved his finger round the dial as though he were counting hours.

"What is it?" demanded Sharpless, in a high voice. "You know something. What is it?"

"Steady, son!"

"You know something you won't tell me," cried the other. He strode forward and seized H.M.'s shoulder. "You're keeping something back; but by God you're going to tell me. What is it? What is it?"

H.M. shook off the hand.

"If I tell you what I think it may be, can you be steady enough to help and not hinder?"

"Yes. Well?"

H.M. gave it to him straight between the eyes.

"Blood-poisoning," he said. "Tetanus. Lockjaw. A nasty way to die."

Eleven

Distantly, a church clock in the town struck the half hour after ten.

In the front garden of Arthur Fane's house, a warm-looking and misty moon penetrated the elms to illumine two figures who were standing on the lawn, glancing up at intervals towards the left-hand bedroom windows. These windows were closed and their curtains drawn, since in tetanus cases no breath of wind must touch the victim lest it bring on convulsions.

Outside in the street stood Dr. Nithsdale's car, and the hospital car which had brought the antitoxic serum.

Ann Browning and Phil Courtney, together on the lawn, spoke in whispers.

"But is there any chance?" Ann muttered. "That's what I want to know. Is there any chance?"

"I can't tell you. I seem to remember reading that if the symptoms come on very quickly, you're a goner."

She put her hand, a warm soft hand, on his arm. She tightened her fingers, and shook the arm fiercely. He had never felt closer to her than in this darkness, where her face looked pallid, her lips dark, and her eyes larger.

"But a little *pin?*" she insisted. "A little thing like a pin, to do all that?"

"It can and has. And it was pressed in to the head, remember."

She shuddered. "Thank heaven *I* didn't use it. Poor Vicky!"

He pressed the hand on his arm.

"I didn't even notice," she said, "that the pin was—rusty."

"It wasn't rusty." He recalled the picture. "I remember how it shone when the light touched it. But then this germ's in the air, in dust; it comes from dust. From anything."

Again she shuddered. A light sprang up in the long windows of the front bedroom across the hall from Vicky's. A long shadow, that of Hubert Fane, crossed and recrossed the windows, beating its hands together. From the house they heard no noise or voice.

"Look here," Courtney said sharply. "You're worrying yourself to death. You can't do any good out here, just watching a closed window. Go in and sit down. H.M. will tell us when there's any news."

"You—you think I'd better?"

"Definitely."

"The trouble is," she burst out, "that Vicky's such a *decent* person. Always trying to do the right thing, always putting herself out for someone else. It just seems as though there's been nothing but trouble, trouble, trouble for her ever since two nights ago, when we first saw . . ."

The front gate clicked.

Dr. Richard Rich, in a somewhat theatrical-looking soft black hat and a dark blue suit, closed the gate behind him and came hesitantly up the path.

"Miss Browning, isn't it?" he inquired, peering in the gloom. "And Mr.—?"

"Courtney."

"Ah, yes! Courtney. Sir Henry's secretary." Rich

rubbed his cheek. "I hope you'll excuse this intrusion. I came to see whether there were any developments."

"Developments!" breathed Ann.

"I beg your pardon?"

"Dr. Rich," said Ann with cruel clearness, "I don't know how many people you've killed, through carelessness, in the course of your professional career. But you killed Vicky Fane last night. She's dying, do you hear? *Dying*."

Rich appeared to be staring back at them through the distorting moonlight.

"What in the name of sanity are you talking about?"

"Steady, Ann!" said Courtney. He put his arm round her shoulders tightly. All her body seemed to droop. "Doctor, do you remember showing Mrs. Fane was really hypnotized by driving a pin into her arm?"

"Yes? Well?"

"Tetanus. The doctors are upstairs with her now."

There was a pause, while they heard him draw in his breath. Then Rich's bass voice hit back like a blow of commonsense directness, with fear behind it.

"That's impossible!"

"Don't take my word for it. Go in and see."

"I tell you it's impossible! The pin was perfectly clean. Besides—"

Rich pulled the brim of his hat still further down. After a pause, during which his mouth seemed to be working, he turned round and started for the house. They followed him. The front door was on the latch, and a light burned in the hall. Rich's mottled pallor was still further revealed as he removed his hat.

"May I go upstairs?"

"I doubt if they'd let you in. The doctors are there, and a man from Scotland Yard."

Rich hesitated. There was a light in the library, at the front and to their left. Motioning to the others to precede him, Rich went in and closed the door.

This library, you felt, was seldom used. It had a correct air of weightiness: a claw-footed desk, a globe-map, and an overmantel of heavy carved wood. The books, clearly bought by the yard and unread, occupied two walls: in their contrasts of brown, red, blue, and black leather or cloth among the sets, even in an occasional artistic gap along the shelves, they showed the hand of the decorator. A bronze lamp burned on the desk.

"Now," Rich said through his teeth. "Please tell me the symptoms."

Courtney told him.

"And these symptoms came on when?"

"Just before tea-time, I understand."

"God in heaven!" muttered Rich, as though unable to believe his ears. He massaged his forehead, and then hastily consulted his watch. "Sixteen hours! Only sixteen hours! I can't believe it would have got as bad as that in only . . ."

His voice grew bewildered, almost piteous.

"I forget," he added. "I have not practiced medicine for eight years. Your knowledge grows scrambled. You . . ." His eyes wandered round the bookshelves. "I don't suppose they'd have any medical works here? Stop. There's a Britannica, at least. It might help to jog my memory."

The set of the Encyclopædia Britannica, fourteenth edition, was on a rather high shelf. Rich stood on tiptoe and plucked down the twenty-first volume, "SORD to TEXT." He carried it to the desk under the lamp. His hands shook. But it was unnecessary for him to leaf through in order to find the article on tetanus.

An envelope, used as a book-mark, was already in the volume at the page containing the tetanus article.

"Somebody's been looking it up already," he observed, flattening out the book.

"Nothing in that," said Ann. "Maybe someone

wanted to know—how bad it was. It's convulsions, isn't it?"

"In the final stages, yes. Excuse me."

"And *you* did it," said Ann.

"Young woman," said Rich, raising a quietly haggard face as his finger followed the words of the text, "I have had much trouble in my life. I don't deserve this."

The door opened, and Sir Henry Merrivale lumbered in.

H.M., still wearing his white flannels and shirt, had his big fists on his hips. His manner had grown even more uneasy. Ann and Courtney regarded him questioningly.

"No better," he growled. "If anything, a little worse. And goin' on." His scowl deepened. "Y'know," he seemed to be speaking to himself rather than to the others, "I'm glad I didn't have the responsibility for diagnosin'. Every symptom exact; rusty pin on dressing table . . . Oh, Lord love a duck, what's *wrong*?"

"Sir Henry!" said Rich sharply.

H.M. woke up.

"Hullo. You here, son?"

"In time—" Rich closed up the book with a bang—"to hear that I'm supposed to be in trouble again. But I tell you frankly, I don't propose to be—what is the word?—framed for the second time. I don't believe it! Fourteen hours! No, sixteen hours; but it's the same. Those symptoms came on too quickly."

"I know, son," agreed H.M., expelling his breath. "That's what worries me too."

Rich's eyes narrowed.

"I wasn't aware you were a medical man, sir."

"Uh-huh. Yes. In a small way.'

"What have they done?"

"Tetanus antitoxin. . . ."

"How much?"

"A thousand units. Injected intrathecally by lumbar puncture. Morphia for the pain. Quiet and dark. What else can they do? And yet, d'ye know—!"

H.M. wandered across the room. He lowered his big bulk of fifteen stone into a carved chair, where he sat glowering.

"When you get to thinkin' about it," he went on, "you can see the symptoms, the real bad symptoms, came on too quick. Unless, of course—" he spoke slowly—"that pin had been dipped into tetanus bacilli to begin with."

The library was so quiet that they could all hear the creaking footsteps which tiptoed in Vicky Fane's bedroom just overhead. It was a physical quality of stillness; it took listeners by the throat. Rich took a step away from the desk. Rich struck his right hand on the globe-map, setting the globe spinning like their wits.

"Are you suggesting," he said, "deliberate murder?"

"I dunno, son. Hardly seems probable, does it? But that'd seem the only explanation. Unless—"

H.M. stopped abruptly. His expression grew fixed and far away, his hand poised in the air. An incredulous look began to dawn behind the big spectacles. He snapped his fingers.

"Excuse me," he muttered hastily, and hauled himself up from the chair. "I got to go."

He was out of the room, and the door had closed behind him, before anyone could speak. They heard his footsteps in the hall.

"Tetanus baccilli," murmured Ann. Her own look was startled, incredulous, and frightened. "But that couldn't be!" She appealed to Rich. "Could it?"

"Don't ask me. I refrain, Miss Browning, from pointing out—" About to say something else, Rich paused. "There's a trap here," he added.

"Doctor?"

"Yes?"

"If Vicky's going to die, when will she die?"

"How can I tell? Death from tetanus rarely takes place within twenty-hours after the onset.

Ann looked at the closed door.

"Twenty-four hours," she repeated. "Five o'clock in the morning. Dawn. Breakfast-time, maybe. Oh, it's horrible!"

Rich said nothing more. Without a glance at them he quietly left the library.

The minutes dragged on. With an instinct of neatness, Ann replaced the volume of the encyclopedia on its shelf.

"I think I'll go home," she decided in a colorless voice. "There's nothing I can do here, and I've got to be up early tomorrow morning. Will you—will you walk part of the way with me?"

"I'll walk all the way with you."

"I go out the back. It's only in Drayton Road, near here. You go up Elm Lane, behind the house, and turn into Old Bath Road."

With no foreboding of what was to come within the next half-hour, Courtney opened the door for her. They tiptoed across the hardwood floor of the hall to the dining room. Some sort of subdued argument now seemed to be going on in the hall upstairs. Two words, "continuous contraction," emerged in H.M.'s voice, followed by the fierce shushing tones of Dr. Nithsdale.

The dining room was dark, but the white-tiled kitchen beyond was lighted. A clock ticked with homely effect on a shelf over the refrigerator. Daisy Fenton, her eyes red with weeping, sat rigidly on a kitchen chair and occasionally wiped her eyes with a corner of her apron.

By the sink stood a stout gray-haired woman whom Courtney supposed to be Mrs. Propper, the cook. Though she held herself like a grenadier, her own eyeballs had a strained look which indicated emotion not far off.

A swing door (which, unexpectedly, did not creak at all) admitted Ann and Courtney to this warm domestic interior.

"Good evening, Mrs. Propper," Ann said politely.

"Evening, Miss Ann."

"You're up late."

"First time I've been out of me bed after nine o'clock," declared Mrs. Propper, balancing herself with one hand on the drain-board, "since that grand dinner-party when they wanted the bomb-a-la-rain for a sweet. (Oh, Daisy, do stop sniveling; there's a good girl!) Miss Ann, who's that wild man?"

"What wild man?"

"That man with the bald head."

"You mean Dr. Rich?"

"Oh, *him?* Not that hypnotist fellow. I know *him.* He came walking through here only a few minutes ago, and out the back door to the garden, without so much as by-your-leave. No, I mean the other man. Big stout man in his shirt-sleeves, if you please, who came in before the hypnotist, and started asking all the questions."

"You mean Sir Henry Merrivale?"

Mrs. Propper was taken aback.

"Lord! Got a title, has he?" Visibly, H.M.'s stock shot up in her estimation. "Now whoever would 'a' thought it? No offense meant, I'm sure. But he did carry on like as if he wasn't right in the head. And then there's that Captain Sharpless. I say it's a disgrace!"

"Auntie!" cried Daisy. "Auntie!"

"I say it's a *disgrace*," affirmed Mrs. Propper, whacking her hand down on the drain-board. "And I'm sure Miss Ann agrees with me. Him coming here the day after, with Mr. Fane not cold in his coffin. And going up to Mrs. Fane's bedroom: her bedroom, if you please: at four o'clock in the afternoon. He's out in the garden now, and I say it's a disgrace."

"Really, Mrs. Propper—!" said Ann.

But, since she refused to show grief at death or illness, Mrs. Propper took it out in another way. The tears did start to her eyes with the strength of her opinions here.

"Mind you, Miss Ann, I'll not say Mr. Fane was all I like a gentleman to be. He did look at my household accounts as though he thought I might cheat him, and tick off every little thing with a pencil. I like a gentleman to be free with his money, or else why *is* he a gentleman?"

"Mrs. Propper, please!"

"But speak no ill of the dead: that's what I've always been taught, and what I always say. There's Mr. Hubert now. Not that he's free with *his* money, but at least it's always a good word and a, 'Surely that's a lot of trouble for you, Mrs. Propper?' You don't mind it," continued the cook, with her jaws working and the tears now running down her face, "if you're appreciated in this world. But speak no ill of the dead; and, after all, he *was* her lawfully wedded husband—"

This was having its effect on Ann.

Courtney, powerfully embarrassed, was afraid that this might end in an orgy with all three of them weeping. And another idea had come to him as well.

"Mrs. Propper!" he snapped, in so sharp and peremptory a tone that she instinctively straightened up.

"Yes, sir?"

"You said that Sir Henry Merrivale was here asking you some questions?"

"Yes, he was."

"Questions about what?"

He roused a new grievance.

"About what food Mrs. Fane had eaten today, that's what."

"Oh?"

"Yes, it is. When Daisy here can tell you that not a mouthful of food has passed her lips today, not a mouthful, except the grapefruit that Captain Sharpless took up to her at four o'clock in the afternoon. That's all she'll ever touch when she feels poorly (as you very well know, Miss Ann), and a thousand times I've told her that it's no food to keep body and soul together."

"Yes, of course, Mrs. Propper, but—"

"And anyway, when the poor lady's dying, in convulsions they say, then what I say is, what difference does it make what she did or didn't eat? That's what *I* say."

fruit trees drooping above. On the other side, a line of elms closed it in as well, with a screen of bushes and stinging-nettles underneath. An apple had fallen here and there, to rot. It was a narrow little lane, in daytime haunted by wasps and at night full of an eerie oppressiveness.

Courtney watched her print frock move away from him and disappear.

He moved back from the gate, and felt in his pocket after his pipe. Hot tonight. Uncomfortably hot. He hadn't noticed this before.

Far away to his left, Leckhampton Hill rose against the moonlit sky, with the clay face of the quarry along its upper ridges. It was the beginning of the Cotswolds, and from it you could see Cheltenham like a gray toy town in the valley. Through Courtney's mind, incongruously, ran lines of verse her remembered having read in an anthology long ago . . .

> *November evenings, damp and still,*
> *That used to deck Leckhampton Hill,*
> *And bring queer winds like harlequins*
> *that seize our elms for violins . . .*

Well, it wasn't November now. No; it was hot. Infernally hot, and the little grass-carpeted lane lay like a tunnel under the over-ripe fruit along the walls.

Phil Courtney filled and lighted his pipe. The little core of light from the match startled him, like a pigmy explosion, when he struck it. He turned back towards the house, realizing that when a match flame made you jump there must be something wrong with your nerves.

Subdued activity seemed to be pulsing in the house. He could tell that, even at this distance away.

He thought of Vicky Fane, pretty, healthy Vicky, with her jaw-muscles rigid as though in a cast, the skin drawn back in the agony of the *risus sardonicus*, lying on a bed which must not be disturbed or even creak in case it brought on the convulsions.

And he had taken a few more steps when he stopped. He heard, distantly, a sound which carried clearly on the still air in these still streets. It might have been a symbol. It was the hurrying clang of an ambulance-bell.

Simultaneously, from somewhere far up the grass lane, a woman began to scream.

Sparks and fire from his pipe spilled to the ground. He tried to knock it out, but thrust it into his pocket without thinking further of it. Subconscious fear returned. The screams, shrill and terrified, were choked off as though by a hand. Then silence, and one more scream.

His fingers were so clumsy that it seemed minutes before he could get the gate open. But he did not hesitate about the direction in which to go. He ran towards the left, his foot sending flying a spongy apple as he ran.

"Ann!" he called. *"Ann!"*

No reply.

"Ann!"

Somewhere ahead of him, he thought he heard a movement; then a pause of what can only be called awareness, and a tearing sound as though of bushes or stinging-nettles.

Only patches of moonlight penetrated the dank, spongy-soft tunnel. He was some hundred yards or more along the lane when he saw her, or at least a huddle in a print frock, leaning on hands and knees near the stone wall to the left. As she seemed to hear his footfalls swish in the grass, she scrambled up and began to run as though blindly in the other direction.

"Ann! It's me! Phil Courtney!"

The figure hesitated, stumbled, tottered, and then stood still. She was standing with her back to him, hardly recognizable in the splintered moonlight, when he reached her.

"What's wrong?"

"Nothing. N-nothing!"

He could hear her thin, harsh breathing, shaking the words and stumbling on them with the accents of terror. He struck a match and held it up.

At first she refused to turn round and face him. When she did so, after the first match had burnt down and another was struck, she was smiling—but not very convincingly.

Her thin frock had been ripped down partly from the left shoulder, exposing the white silk slip and outlining the breast. A bruise was beginning to show on her neck under the left ear. Her thick hair, which she wore bound round her head, was slightly loosened; hairpins showed in it. There were grass-stains on her dress at the knees, and on the rumpled tan silk stockings underneath. She was bedraggled, grimy, obviously frightened—but trying to carry it off as though nothing had happened.

"Don't make a noise!" she urged. "I'm p-perfectly all right. Do put out that match. No, don't. Light another."

"But what—"

"It was someone. A man."

"What man?"

"I d-don't know." She passed the back of her hand across her forehead. "He caught me from behind and put his hand over my mouth. He—anyway, I fought loose and yelled. He got his hand on my mouth again. I think I bit his hand, but I'm not sure. When he heard you coming, he must have . . ."

"Where did he go?"

"A-across there, most likely. Towards the fields. It's open fields. No, don't! Don't! Come back!"

The darkness was dense, the stinging-nettles a formidable brush. Striking still another match, he held it above his head. There was nothing else here except the unkempt grass and a decayed plum or two.

"Would you recognize him again?"

"No. I never even saw him. Please! Don't make a row! Take me home."

She was trembling badly now.

Holding her arm in his, he took her along the lane for some three hundred yards, to where faint white street-lamps glimmered in the Old Bath Road.

"I shall be all right now," she assured him. "No, don't come any farther. I don't want my father or mother to see you; and I don't want them to see me either; or heaven knows what they'd think. Good night. And thanks."

She was gone, running lightly and holding up the shoulder of her torn frock, before he had time to protest. He saw her turn in at a gate near by, with a quick look up and down the road. Then, more violently disturbed than ever before in his life, Phil Courtney retraced his steps.

Psychic fits, it seemed, had their uses after all. The episode had been so brief and rapid that he wondered whether he might have dreamed it. Stopping again at the place where he had found Ann, which he had marked by a wooden back gate with a white enameled sign reading, "No hawkers or circulars," he struck matches to see whether any traces might have been left."

No footprints. No convenient cuff-link dropped, or similar clue. Only the trampled grass, the evil lane, the close-pressing elms.

"I'll be a—" he began aloud.

His last match burnt his fingers, and he dropped it. He returned to the Fanes' house and opened the gate, where a shadow rose up in front of him.

But it was only Frank Sharpless.

"Who's there?" demanded Sharpless's voice out of the gloom.

"Me."

"Oh. What time is it?"

"I don't know. Must be past eleven. Frank, have you seen anybody hanging about here?"

It took some little while to make Sharpless understand this question. He seemed dazed, and so completely in anguish that Courtney's concern for Ann was almost lost in pity. He remembered that Vicky Fane was dying of lockjaw up there in an airless room.

"Attacked Ann?" Sharpless kept repeating stupidly. "Where? When? Why" Though he was trying to focus on this, he could not do so. "Was she hurt?"

"No. Only a bruise and a torn dress."

"But was the fellow trying to. . . ?"

"I don't know. Trying to kill her too, more probably."

"What do you mean, trying to 'kill her *too*?' " asked Sharpless, after a pause as though for confused thought.

"Nothing. Just a slip of speech."

Sharpless's powerful fingers fastened on his arm. "You don't think anybody tried to kill Vicky? Not deliberately?"

"No, no, no!"

"I hear you've fallen for Ann."

"Yes. I have."

"Good luck, old boy. I'd be more congratulatory, only at a time like this . . ." In the dimness he swept his arm towards the house. He stiffened. His tone altered, and his voice deepened. All his heart was in it. "Don't let her die," he said. "Dear God, don't let her die!"

"Steady."

"But what are they doing up there, anyway? Something's up. I know it. More people came from the hospital or somewhere. But they won't even let me in. Wait! I forgot to ask you. What time is it?"

"You did ask me. I said—"

Distantly, the church clock answered them by beginning to strike.

"Only twelve?" demanded Sharpless in an incredulous voice. He had whirled round after counting the first three. "Only midnight? Cripes, it can't be. There's something wrong with that clock. It's two o'clock in the morning, or more. It must be."

"Frank, you've got to get hold of yourself."

"I tell you, there's something wrong with that clock!"

But there was nothing wrong with the clock.

They discovered this long before its clang had struck the quarter, the half-hour, the three-quarter, and the hour again.

In Sharpless's present frame of mind, Courtney thought it best to keep him away from the house, in case he made a scene. He sat Sharpless down on a stone bench under the trees. He got him to smoking cigarettes. The lights of the house burned more brightly as those of the town died; and still no word came from the sick-room upstairs.

The clang of the church clock got into their thoughts. They heard it when it did not strike, and were startled by it when it did.

While the hours dragged on, Sharpless talked. He talked monotonously, quickly, in a low voice which rarely varied in key. He talked of himself and Vicky Fane. Of what they were going to do when she was well. Of what he was going to do at Staff College. He said he might be sent out to India, and gave a long description of life in India. He quoted his father and his uncles and his grandfather for this.

Dawn, Courtney thought, could not be far off. It would come white and ghostly among the fruit trees.

The church clock struck two-thirty.

Ten minutes later, while Sharpless was recalling an interminable childhood and a game called Little Wars, the back door of the house opened.

"Captain Sharpless!" called Mrs. Propper's voice. It poured with acid. "Captain Sharpless!"

With Courtney following him, Sharpless ran.

"They think you'd better go in," said Mrs. Propper gravely.

"Steady, Frank!"

"I can't face it," said Sharpless. "I can't!"

"You've got to. Damn it, don't turn into a weak sister now! Go on."

Sharpless walked slowly through the kitchen, past a blubbering Daisy. He stumbled over a chair in the dining room, and only found his way out when Courtney switched on the lights.

In the downstairs hall, a little group was stumping down the stairs: with many pauses, as though nobody could drag himself away from the room above. First came little Dr. Nithsdale, then Sir Henry Merrivale, and then a man in a white coat. But what struck Courtney like a blow across the skull was the expressions on their faces.

The man in the white coat, though his forehead looked damp with perspiration, was smiling. H.M. had a heavy, sour glare of relief. Even Dr. Nithsdale, though a fierce-looking little man with a bedside manner which would have alarmed Methuselah, appeared less assertive than usual.

His voice was low but penetrating and shrill.

"Mind," he said, "I'll no' say it wasna a bonny guess! Ye've Sco'ish blood in ye're veins, I hae nae doot. Hoots, dinna trouble tae deny it! But I'll no' say, either, mind you, that the leddy's oot o' danger or owt like it, until—"

He paused. His eye fell on Sharpless, who was standing by the newel-post.

"Hoots!" said Dr. Nithsdale, stopping short. "Here's a lad could du wi' a dose o' physic! Losh, mon, hauld tight! Ye're—"

"Is she dead?"

"Hoots!" said Dr. Nithsdale, with rich scorn.

It was H.M. who answered. He steadied Sharpless as the latter put both hands on the rail of the staircase.

"It's all right, son," H.M. said gently. "Take it easy. She'll live."

Thirteen

Friday passed, and Saturday. It was Sunday afternoon before Chief Inspector Masters, who had been very busy in the meantime, again called for a conference with Sir Henry Merrivale.

Philip Courtney had also been busy.

He had now taken down about ninety thousand words of the memoirs. Of these, after matter libelous, scandalous, or in bad taste had been removed, he estimated that roughly a fifth would be publishable. He was well satisfied. This would keep the book in proportion; and he was in no hurry to get it done.

Some anecdotes it cut him to the heart to strike out. One was a vivid and realistic account of H.M.'s first serious love-affair, at the age of sixteen. But as the lady concerned was now the wife of a Cabinet Minister, noted throughout England for her pious works, he judged it best omitted.

The other was a particularly fiendish trick—H.M.'s technique seemed to improve with his advancing years—devised for the discomfiture of Uncle George. But, since it concerned a certain use to which not even Satan himself would think to put a lavatory, Courtney regretfully omitted it as well.

Dictation, too, was difficult. They were not interrupted by the inquest, which was held on Saturday and adjourned at the request of the police after Arthur Fane's body had been formally identified by Hubert.

But they were interrupted by H.M.'s sudden passion for visiting chemists' shops.

Courtney would not have believed there were so many chemists in the world, let alone Cheltenham. He knew, of course, that something was up. If H.M. had gone about showing photographs for identification, or asking pertinent questions about people, he could have understood it. But H.M. did none of these things.

He would go into the shop, ask for a prescription of one sort or another to be made up, and loiter for a ten minutes' chat about nothing while the chemist filled it. No name was mentioned, no question asked.

As a result, H.M.'s purchases were accumulating. Their number and variety would have been regarded with envy by the man in Uncle George's arithmetic-sums. They moved even Major Adams, H.M.'s host, to remonstrance.

"But dammit, my dear chap!" expostulated the major. "After all, I mean to say, dammit!"

"What's wrong, son?"

"Well, if you feel you must haunt chemists' shops, why don't you buy something useful? Shaving soap? Razor blades? Tooth paste? To date," said the major, counting, "you've bought fourteen bottles of cough mixture, twelve bottles of soothing syrup, nine bottles of horse liniment, eight bottles of—"

"You let me alone, son. I know what I'm doing."

And Courtney had to assume he did.

Courtney did not see Ann between Thursday and Sunday. She had gone back to her ordinary work at Gloucester, and his evenings were too occupied with the dictation to see her then.

On Sunday—a heavy, muggy day which threatened rain—he was for once depressed to see that H.M. had wound himself up for a garrulous spell of reminiscing. And he welcomed the interruption when Chief Inspector Masters arrived soon after lunch.

Masters found H.M. in the library, in carpet-slippers, with his feet up on the desk, immersed in a curious anecdote about the Davenport brothers and their use of a lazy-tongs in the middle-'eighties. He kept his eyes shut until he had finished this. Then he looked very hard at Masters, and abandoned all pretense of dictating by saying:

"Yes? Any news?"

Masters's face was very grim.

"Plenty," the chief inspector assured him. "Mrs. Fane is much better, and able to take notice. And it's just as well she is. For I'm bound to admit there does seem to be something in that Polly Allen business."

"Aha!"

Masters, though his heightened color showed what he really thought of it, was cautious.

"We can't bank on it," he warned. "Not yet. Though I'll get the truth out of Mrs. Fane today or I'm a Dutchman. But Agnew and I talked to any number of people who know—or knew—Polly Allen."

"Good. One of the gals, was she?"

Masters spread out his notebook on the desk.

"If you mean professional, no. Not by a jugful!"

"So? That's very interestin'."

"She hung about bars a good deal, it's true. She'd let anybody stand her a drink. But she was very—choosy. Liked 'em young, and didn't care a hang about money. That hardly seems human, but there you are. Quite the lady, in a small way."

"What did she do for a living?"

Masters frowned.

"Nobody seems quite to know. She hadn't any of what you'd call pals. Just a few hello-what-terrible-weather-isn't-it acquaintances. She told 'em she was on the stage for a while. . . ."

"On the stage? Doin' what?"

"She didn't say. Very mysterious and hoity-toity about it, though. We can look her up through the theatrical agencies, if you think it's worth while. I've got a snapshot of her."

From between the pages of his notebook Masters drew out a small photograph. H.M. took his feet down off the desk and studied it. Masters and Courtney looked over his shoulder.

It was a snapshot taken at the seaside. It showed a slim girl, perhaps nineteen years old, in an extremely scanty flowered bathing suit. She was standing on a crowded beach, laughing, her arms up as though she were about to catch a beach ball. Taken in strong sun and with a steady camera, every detail was vividly limned: the gleaming dark hair, the full lips, the rounded nose.

H.M. spoke abruptly.

"I say, Masters. Doesn't she remind you of somebody?"

"Can't say she does, sir."

"Somebody we've seen recently? For the love of Esau, think!" persisted H.M. He turned to Courtney. "What about you?"

Courtney nodded. He had his own emotional reasons for seeing the likeness.

"She's a little like Ann Browning. The color of the hair is different, but the features and the expression—"

Masters looked doubtful.

"Oh, ah. I suppose she is, a bit. But what of it? Anything there, do you think?"

What Courtney was thinking, with a return of all his old apprehensions, was that what had happened to Polly Allen in July might have happened to Ann

Browning Thursday night. He had told H.M. about this attack, and it had been received with a significant silence which disturbed him still more.

H.M. now pushed the snapshot to the middle of the desk-blotter. Again H.M. remained silent for a time, twiddling his thumbs.

"Humph. Well. Go on about Polly Allen."

"She was last seen alive," pursued Masters, consulting his notebook, "about eight o'clock on the night of July fifteenth."

"Ho! Just what the Browning gal suggested?"

"Yes, sir. Polly Allen had a drink with two girl-friends in the bar at the Queen's Hotel—I gather that's the swankiest place in town—and said she couldn't stay, because she had a 'heavy date.' "

"Was this affair with Arthur Fane pretty well known?"

"No. She seems to have kept it dark. That's natural enough. Her friends say she seemed pretty gay about something ('amused,' was what they said). Out she went about eight o'clock, and hasn't been seen by anybody since.

"She had a bed-sitting-room over a shop in the Promenade. Her things are still there. But, since her rent was paid to the end of the month and she had a habit of mooching off like that without saying boo to anybody, the landlady didn't worry."

Masters's color grew still more florid.

"Now, mind!" he insisted. "That don't necessarily mean she's dead. But I'm bound to admit . . ."

"Yes. Exactly."

All of them were silent for a time. In that thick, muggy day, occasional sunlight glimmered on the collection of old weapons hung round the library walls. H.M. scowled still more.

"Any other evidence you've dug up?"

Masters turned to another page.

"Hurrum! To carry on. After a lot of trouble with the bank, we've looked up the financial positions of everybody concerned. And there's nothing there either to help us or surprise us.

"Arthur Fane's will, as I think I told you, leaves everything unconditionally to his wife, and to selected charities if anything happens to her. He's the only Fane in the firm of Fane, Fane & Randall; his father died a long time ago, and his mother in 1929. His estate consists of the house in Fitzherbert Avenue, which he owns; a little life insurance; and, when things are settled up, about two thousand in cash. Not much of a haul for Mrs. Fane there."

Phil Courtney sat up.

"Hoy!" he protested.

Both the others blinked at him.

"What's the matter, son?"

"When I was in that damned bedroom on the night of all the mess," he explained, "I happened to see Fane's bank book. There was twenty-two hundred pounds in his current account alone."

He detailed the incident, but Masters was not impressed.

"That's just about correct," the chief inspector agreed. "It's debts I'm talking about. I've seen the figures. Most of the cash was in the current account: maybe so he could get at it easy if he had to have it in a hurry. Some people intimate that there's been something very, very fishy about the firm of Fane, Fane & Randall. We know Mr. Fane had to sell his life insurance about six months ago, but he got it all back.

"And, whatever money he had to pay out, it's all covered up now. Mr. Fane was a very conscientious sort of bloke. His books are in order, and everything as neat as a pin."

"They couldn't," said Courtney, "be as neat as a certain pin *I'm* thinking about."

"Eh?"

All the repressed curiosity of the past three days, all the ache and memory of that night in the garden with Vicky Fane struggling for life, came back in a wave of almost maniacal bewilderment.

"Look here," Courtney said, "I've got no concern with this case, except that a friend of mine does happen to be mixed up in it. It may be none of my business. But may I ask just one question?"

"Sure, son," conceded H.M. "Fire away."

"Then what is all this funny business about the tetanus poisoning? I know there's something wrong and fishy about the whole thing. I know it's not what you expected. But I can't quite tell where or what the funny business is. Like this. On Wednesday night, about eleven o'clock, Dr. Rich jabbed a pin into Vicky Fane's arm up in that bedroom. Correct?"

H.M. and Masters exchanged glances. After a suggestion of a shrug, and an almost imperceptible nod, the chief inspector seemed to be handing the matter over to H.M.'s discretion.

H.M. sniffed.

"You ought to know, son. You saw it."

"Right. I saw it. About sixteen hours later, violent symptoms of advanced tetanus come on. Correct?"

"Correct."

"You go dashing over to the house, take a look at Vicky Fane, and in a glass tray on the dressing table of the bedroom you find a rusty pin. I understood you to say so, anyway, on Thursday night. Is that correct too?"

"It is."

"Well," continued Courtney, inflating his chest, "I can testify for one that the pin Rich stuck into Vicky Fane's arm was ruddy well *not* rusty. I don't know whether it was infected, or had bacilli on it. But it wasn't rusty, because I remember seeing it shine when he handled it.

"Now what I want to know is: what is all this? What's the catch? When you did all that running about, and finger-snapping, and arguing with the doctors, what did it mean?"

H.M. sighed.

"It meant, son, that we were on the edge of makin' a blinkin' awful mistake."

"Mistake?"

"Yes. Which the murderer wanted us to make. And which was as neat as anything you ever saw.

"Y'see, the murderer knew about that pin-jabbing episode. It was manna from heaven. So the murderer simply dropped a rusty pin on the dressing table, did a certain thing on the followin' day, and let nature take its course.

"Any doctor, hearin' the circumstances, seeing the symptoms, and inevitably coming across that pin, would be bound to diagnose tetanus. When Mrs. Fane died, it would be a regrettable accident. Richard Rich, the disgraced one, would again be held responsible. His carelessness would be supposed to have done it. There would be no suspicion and no post-mortem. Consequently . . ."

Courtney passed a hand across his forehead.

"Wait! For the love of Mike, wait! Then what *was* wrong with the pin Rich jabbed in her arm?"

"Nothing."

"Nothing?"

H.M. seemed bothered by an invisible fly.

"Haven't you guessed it yet, son?" he inquired. "What ailed Mrs. Fane wasn't tetanus at all. It was strychnine poisoning."

Fourteen

Phil Courtney got to his feet.

"Strychnine—" he began.

Taking a somewhat crumpled cigar from his pocket, H.M. bit off the end, expectorated the end neatly across into the fireplace, and lit the cigar. Its smoke hung round his head in an oily cloud.

"The point is," he explained, "that the symptoms of tetanus are exactly the same as the symptoms of strychnine poisoning, except that the effects of strychnine come on a whole lot quicker. The only slight difference is in the nature of the cramps—the muscles are in a continuous state o' contraction for tetanus—but nothing that would bother the keenest doctor if he'd already got tetanus in his mind."

H.M. blew out smoke somberly.

"It wasn't us that saved Mrs. Fane's life, son," he added. "It was only the fact that the murderer gave her too big a dose. It was so whackin' big that it neutralized itself. Once I sent for a stomach-pump . . ."

Courtney, without seeing him, stared at the past. It was as though many blurred pictures had now come into focus to form a series.

"Nice pleasant gentleman or lady, this murderer,"

observed Masters grimly. "Oh, ah! You've got a bit of a better idea now, haven't you, Mr. Courtney?"

Courtney had.

"Just a minute!" he begged. "When was the strychnine given to her, then?"

"About four o'clock on Thursday afternoon, we make it," replied Masters. "That's to say: about twenty minutes before the symptoms started to come on. Strychnine usually begins to work within twenty minutes."

"I see. And it was administered through the mouth, wasn't it? In a grapefruit?"

H.M. raised his eyebrows.

"So?" he grunted, peering round a poisonous cloud of smoke. "Have you been tryin' to play detective too? But that's right. It must 'a' been the grapefruit. First, the cook swears it's the only thing Mrs. Fane ate on Thursday. Second, grapefruit's one of the few things that'd be bitter enough of itself to hide the bitter taste of strychnine—drat him!"

"Drat who?"

"This feller who's been foolin' us!" roared H.M. "*I* was the one who led everybody up the garden path. *I* was the one who fell into the trap, as smooth and slick as you please, and started babblin' about tetanus. It's small thanks to me Mrs. Fane's alive now. Cor!"

"Have you found the grapefruit that was used?"

It was Masters who answered him.

"No, sir, we haven't. And we're not likely to. At the time we had other things to think about—Mrs. Fane. When Sir Henry asked the cook later, she said she'd thrown the grapefruit in the dustbin. It wasn't there when we looked. Naturally. Somebody'd removed it."

Masters drew a design on the edge of his notebook with his pencil. His boiled eye looked wicked. He added sinister curlicues to the design, and said:

"It's not likely the murderer'd go poking about a

dustbin in broad daylight. Especially as the dustbin's by that garden shed near the back door. Too conspicuous. So it'll be very interesting to know, sir, who was hanging about that back garden after dark."

Courtney thought back.

"It'll also be a good thing to know," continued Masters, scoring black lines, "who was hanging about when Mrs. Propper prepared the grapefruit. And who could have got at it. *And* who carried it up to Mrs. Fane."

"But it certainly wasn't—"

Courtney began this sentence with a rush, and checked himself. Two pairs of eyes fastened on him.

"Yes, sir?" Masters prompted blandly. "You were saying?"

He tried to cough up a laugh.

"I was going to say, it certainly wasn't Frank Sharpless, of all people. The idea of him poisoning Mrs. Fane is so fantastic that you hardly need to consider it."

Masters was noncommittal.

"Just so. Evidently. And if that young gentleman isn't careful, he's going to be asked to resign his commission. Still, evidence is evidence."

"And what is more," said Courtney, "it doesn't lessen the troubles you're already in. You've already proved conclusively that nobody could have exchanged the daggers on Wednesday night. If you now prove that nobody could have poisoned the grapefruit on Thursday afternoon, you *will* be in the soup for fair."

He had meant nothing by this. But Masters' color, from being ruddy, threatened to turn purple. Masters had been compelled to cork himself down for so long that the bare suggestion of this possibility was almost enough to finish him.

Snapping a rubber band round his notebook, he drew a deep breath and got up. He began to walk up and down under the lines of old weapons, which he regarded lovingly as though they expressed his mood.

"Now see here," he began firmly. "I'm done with flum-diddling and funny business—"

"You think so?" inquired H.M. "Cor!"

"I tell you, I'm done with flum-diddling and funny business. I'm fair sick of the word 'impossible.' I don't ever want to hear it again. What's impossible about this? Poison in a grapefruit. Well?"

H.M. soothed him.

"Steady on, Masters. I'll just bet you you're not really thinkin' about impossibilities at all. You're thinkin' about your great big beautiful case against Mrs. Fane. Now aren't you?"

"That's as may be, sir."

"Aren't you? Because, son, that case is shot to blazes. She wouldn't be likely to give herself strychnine just to prove she died of tetanus. Now would she?"

Masters did not say anything. But he cast longing eyes at a murderous-looking Malay kris on the wall.

H.M. smoked reflectively.

"I was just wonderin'. If we eliminate Mrs. Fane, subject to change of mind without notice, is there anybody else we can eliminate?"

Masters was emphatic about this.

"No, there is not. In one of your cases, I wouldn't eliminate the Pope or the Archbishop of Canterbury. Whoever you think it can't be, that's always the person it is. What were you going to say, though?"

"I was just thinkin' about Dr. Rich."

"To tell you the truth, sir, so was I."

"Here's a chap," argued H.M., "who's had a lot laid at his door he's not guilty of. That business with the alleged rusty pin, for instance. The poor feller must have gone nearly out of his mind Thursday night."

"Oh, ah," acknowledged Masters. "*And* no motive."

"And, so far as appears, no motive. What do you think, son?"

"I think," snapped Masters, taking up his hat, "that

we've done enough talking. I think that the sooner we cut along there and see Mrs. Fane and the cook, the sooner we can argue as much as we like. Are you ready, Sir Henry? And you, sir? Then what are we waiting for?"

Ten minutes later, when H.M. had been persuaded to put on a coat, they were ringing the front door bell at the Fanes'.

The door was opened by an effulgent Daisy, whose snub nose and freckled face shone as though they had been polished. Masters greeted her with a smile that was confidential and bland.

"*Good* afternoon, miss."

"Good afternoon, sir."

"And how is Mrs. Fane today? Better, I hope?"

"*Ever* so much better, sir," beamed Daisy. The look she directed at H.M. had in it something little short of awe. "She's sitting up a bit, in bed."

"Do you think we might see her, now?"

"I don't see why not, sir. Miss Browning's with her now. But I'll have to go and ask. Will you come in?"

"No hurry, miss. No hurry! As a matter of fact, we'd just like to have a word with Mrs. Propper first. Now, now! Nothing to be alarmed about. Just a little thing where we think she can help us."

"Auntie's in the kitchen. This way, please."

Ann Browning was not upstairs. She was coming down the stairs at this moment, dressed in a white twill sports-frock with bare arms, and with much of the strain gone from her face. The bruise on her neck under the ear must have been covered with powder, for it was not visible.

Masters greeted her genially as she reached the hall.

"Afternoon, Miss Browning! Sorry to hear about that business the other night. You haven't been getting yourself attacked again, have you?"

Ann stopped short.

"You told him!" she said, looking reproachfully at Courtney. "I wish you hadn't!"

"Hang it all, Ann, it might have been serious! You don't seem to realize the danger you were in."

"It was nothing, Mr. Masters," she assured the chief inspector, ignoring this. "Please forget it. I don't want any bother. I—I suppose you've come to see Vicky? Is there anything new?"

Masters adopted an air of jocoseness which Courtney found somewhat heavy.

"Nothing much, miss. Except," he lowered his voice, "you can thank your lucky stars you were sitting on the lawn at Major Adams's place with us at four o'clock in the afternoon on Thursday."

"Why?"

"Ah! Big secret, miss. Very dark. Come along, Sir Henry."

While Ann stared at them perplexedly, Masters and H.M. followed Daisy towards the dining room. Courtney held back to speak to her.

"You didn't," said Ann, with her eyes on the floor, "you didn't ring up or come round on Friday or Saturday. At night, anyway. I was rather hoping you would."

His day, which hitherto had been overcast and threatening rain, suddenly grew dazzling with sun.

"You mean that?"

"Yes. Of course."

"My dear girl," he roared, "if I'd any idea, any idea at all, that you . . . Good God, what's that?"

The noise, it is true, would have made anyone jump. It was due to a variety of circumstances. The dining-room floor was of polished hardwood which did not creak, but was, on the contrary, of exceptional firmness and slipperiness. Round it were scattered a few rugs like islands. It is unwise to step quickly on one of these rugs when you are not looking where you are going. Sir Henry Merrivale had committed this error.

Merely to say that H.M. took a toss conveys nothing. It lacks the element of majesty attendant on what happened.

His feet flew straight out ahead of him as though galvanized. His despairing howl was of no avail. After describing something of an arc, his ample posterior struck the floor with a crash that made the chandelier rattle, and sent him slithering six feet into a china-closet. There was a pause. Then there rose up in his powerful voice such a torrent of profanity, such a flood of blasphemy and vile obscenities, as must have made George Merrivale himself blush in the infernal regions.

"Sh-h!" urged Masters, also galvanized. "No, no, no! Sh-h!"

The kitchen door was flung open, and Mrs. Propper dashed out.

"I won't have such language—"

She broke off abruptly. Something of Daisy's awe had communicated itself even to Mrs. Propper.

"Heaven save us," she breathed, "it's the big doctor."

Only inarticulate gobbling sounds answered her, since Masters had fastened a big hand over H.M.'s mouth.

He removed his hand only when he judged it safe.

"Madam," said H.M. getting his breath but continuing to sit on the floor, "I'd sort of like to suggest that you got your verbs confused. I'm not a big doctor. But I *need* a big doctor. I need him like billy-o."

"I do hope you're not hurt, sir?"

"Hurt? I'm paralyzed! I'm—"

"Would you like me to rub some embrocation on it?"

H.M. merely looked at her.

"Get up, sir!" hissed Masters, in embarrassed despair. He tried to lift H.M., who merely sat stubbornly like a mule until a sudden idea appeared to occur to him.

Then he got up of his own accord, quickly, and went round counting the rugs. His deadly injury seemed to be forgotten.

If on Thursday night Mrs. Propper would merely have called him a wild man, this afternoon she showed no such tendency. To Mrs. Propper, a chastened woman, he was something only a little short of a wizard. He had saved Vicky Fane from dying of lockjaw.

Masters saw it, and resolved to take due advantage.

"Very interestin'!" growled H.M., surveying the room. "Very!" Suddenly he seemed to remember; he groaned, and belatedly affected a bad limp; but, as this impressed nobody—even the anxious Mrs. Propper—he grudgingly discarded it.

"No sympathy," he said. "No sympathy for anybody! Looky here, ma'am. Chief Inspector Masters wants to ask you . . ."

"You ask her, sir," said Masters softly.

"I'm sure if there's anything I can do for you, sir," said Mrs. Propper, "I'd be only too glad to do it! Will you come into the kitchen?"

They went. Ann and Courtney followed. Though Masters seemed about to protest, H.M.'s glare silenced him.

Here H.M. leaned his elbow on the refrigerator.

"Ma'am," he began meditatively, "I'm goin' to deal very frankly with you. Can you keep a secret?"

Mrs. Propper's eyes gleamed.

Through the kitchen windows Courtney could see the dustbin beside the garden shed. Its metal lid was askew, and was now being investigated by a stray cat.

"I'm sure I'll do my best, sir!"

"Good. Now, ma'am, you think Mrs. Fane nearly died of lockjaw. Don't you?"

"Seeing it was you who brought her round, sir . . ."

"Well, she didn't. She was deliberately poisoned with

some stuff called strychnine. That poison was put into a grapefruit, a piece of grapefruit, that you prepared for her about four o'clock on Thursday afternoon. Remember?"

Dead silence, except for the kitchen clock.

If this statement had been made by anybody else in Mrs. Propper's acquaintance, the result would probably have been fury or hysterics. As it was, she merely blinked back at him. It took some time before she even understood. But he ought to know. He was the Big Doctor.

Nor was the effect on Ann Browning less pronounced. Courtney glanced sideways at her tense arms and profile. Otherwise everyone in the kitchen stood rigid.

"God save us," muttered Mrs. Propper, getting her breath, "I—"

"Easy now! We're not suggestin' *you* had anything to do with it. We're sure you didn't. All we say is that somebody tampered with the grapefruit. The poison might 'a' been in the form of a liquid, or of a white powder. You do remember, don't you?"

Mrs. Propper swallowed.

"So help me, sir, *I* don't know nothing about it! I've been a good woman all my life, so help me, and I'd never—"

"Now, now, now! I *said* we know *you* didn't do it! Didn't I say that? All right. I'm just askin': you do remember preparing the grapefruit?"

Mrs. Propper sat down rather abruptly in a white chair. She began in a dazed way to fan her face with her apron. What her manner might be when she had assimilated the shock was difficult to tell.

"Yes, I do indeed. But—"

"What happened?"

The cook searched her wits. "I took the grapefruit out of the ice-box, and cut it in half, and put one half in a nice dish—"

"Uh-huh. But before that?"

"Before when? Oh! I see what you mean. Don't hurry me, sir! Please don't hurry me. Mrs. Fane's bell rang—" wordless, she pointed to the indicator-board on the wall—"and Daisy went up and answered it."

"Yes?"

"Daisy came down, and said Mrs. Fane would like a nice grapefruit. Daisy'll tell you that herself. Though the times I've told Mrs. Fane, the times I've said, it's not enough to keep body and soul together—"

"Go on."

"I took the grapefruit out of—" This time she pointed to the refrigerator.

"It was a whole grapefruit, was it? It wasn't cut already?"

"Oh, no, sir! I cut it myself. With a knife," she added, evidently wanting to be precise.

"Who was here in the kitchen then?"

"Only Daisy and me."

"You're sure of that, now?"

"Only Daisy and me, so help me!"

"All right. What happened to the other half of the grapefruit?"

"I ate it myself."

It was very warm in the kitchen. H.M. peered round and exchanged a glance with Masters.

"Go on from there, ma'am. You cut the grapefruit—"

"Yes. And put it in the glass dish." She made illustrative gestures. "And put it on a nice tray, with a spoon and a little sugar-bowl. And sprinkled some sugar on it."

"So," murmured H.M. "You sprinkled some sugar on it. I just want you to remember, ma'am. Strychnine is a white powder that looks for all the world like sugar. It could have been mixed in with the sugar, couldn't it?"

"Nasty stuff!" said Mrs. Propper, suddenly and violently. "Nasty stuff! No, sir, I swear it couldn't!"

"Couldn't have been in the sugar? Why not?"

She swallowed.

"Because, as soon as I'd sprinkled a little sugar on, I sprinkled a lot of—I mean, I sprinkled some sugar from that same bowl on me own grapefruit. And ate it. And I'm as right as rain."

H.M. turned round and exchanged with Masters a glance which seemed to say, "sunk." Even H.M. was growing rattled. He put up a hand and adjusted his spectacles, cleared his throat, and eyed her again.

"You're sure, now, that nobody—not even Daisy—came near the grapefruit while you were doin' that?"

"Oh, sir, would I lie to you?"

"Don't carry on, now! What happened then?"

Mrs. Propper was transfixed by memory as though by an arrow.

"Then, just then, Captain Sharpless opened the door. He'd been up in Mrs. Fane's room (And there's things the Good Lord won't allow in this world, either, if you ask me!)

"And he said, he said, 'Don't bother, Daisy; I'll take it up to her.' And I handed him the tray." Her eyes were fixed and horrified. She made an illustrative gesture of handing the tray. "And out he walked with it. And so if anybody put that dreadful stuff in the grapefruit . . . God love us, it must have been that Captain Sharpless himself."

Her voice had grown louder, ringing in the kitchen. Footsteps crossed the floor of the dining room beyond. Frank Sharpless, pushing open the swing-door so that it almost caught Ann a blow behind the shoulder, poked his head round the edge of the door.

"Hullo!" he said pleasantly. "Did I hear somebody mention my name?"

Fifteen

"Daisy said you were out here," he went on. "What's the conference all about? Is anything up?"

Mrs. Propper's expression must have betrayed her to anyone who was looking at her. She moved her ample body as though about to utter a stifled shriek. Her wide-open eyes conveyed that she had thought he was wicked, but not this wicked.

Sharpless did not look at her. He was a very different person from the hag-ridden talker of the garden. A clearer picture of (as the Sunday School weeklies would say) youth, health, and innocence could not have been found.

Fresh from shave and hair-cut at the barber's, his hair sleekly groomed, his good-humored smile widening and his eyes untroubled, Sharpless saluted them with his cap. His stick was tucked under his left arm.

Chief Inspector Masters did not step into the breach: he jumped there. Perhaps they were all afraid that Mrs. Propper might leap up and cry, "Murderer!" or some such perfectly sincere melodramatic gesture, making the kitchen explode with emotionalism.

"Just clearing up a few matters, sir," said Masters, in a voice loud with warning to the cook. "You don't happen to remember carrying—what was it?—a *grape-*

fruit, yes! You don't happen to remember carrying half a grapefruit up to Mrs. Fane on Thursday afternoon, do you?"

Sharpless smiled.

"I'll say I do! I remember everything about that afternoon. What about it?"

"Oh, ah. You *did* carry it up, then?"

"Yes, of course. What about it?"

"And you didn't put it down anywhere? Or stop to talk to anybody? You just took it up, and handed it to the lady? *Eh?*"

If Frank's astonishment were assumed, Courtney thought, he must be among the first actors of the world. It was as though you could read every thought in the man's head.

"That's right. And you can add, if you like, that I stopped there and watched her while she ate it." Enlightenment came to him. "Oh! I get it! You're wondering whether the grapefruit might have had a bad effect, or a good effect, in bringing on the poison?"

"Something like that."

"Well," said Sharpless, drawing in his breath, "if it had a good effect, I'm glad. And if it had a bad effect—well, that doesn't matter now, thanks to Sir Henry. I haven't thanked you properly, sir, for whatever it was you did the other night. But, by gad, if there's ever anything you want done for you: a little matter of a murder or anything like that: you just come to me. I'm your man."

"Eee!" cried Mrs. Propper, and flounced up out of her chair like a pouncing owl.

H.M. saved the situation then by deliberately reaching behind Masters, unobserved, and pushing the kitchen clock off the shelf.

It was the sacrifice of a good clock, but it worked.

"She's upset, poor old girl," observed Sharpless sympathetically, watching Mrs. Propper as she tried to conceal her emotion by a distracted examination of broken wheels and springs. "I'm going up to see Vicky. Cheer-ho. See you later."

The swing-door closed.

"My poor little clock!" cried Mrs. Propper. "My *nice* little clock!"

Ann Browning spoke in a low, clear, firm voice.

"Sir Henry," she said, "that boy isn't guilty. You know it as well as I do."

"Why is that man wearing his hat in my house?" demanded Mrs. Propper, gathering up the clock and pointing at Masters. "I won't have him wearing his hat in our house."

Holding himself under strong restraint, Masters walked—he almost tiptoed—to the door leading out into the back garden. He opened this, stood aside, and nodded to the others. H.M., Ann, and Courtney filed out. Masters followed them, and firmly closed the door.

Even the thick, close air outside was welcome after the air of the kitchen.

"Chief Inspector," said Courtney, "I didn't know I was speaking in prophecy. No offense is meant. But, as Ann said, you know as sure as you're born that Frank Sharpless never poisoned a grapefruit to give to Vicky Fane. And if Frank didn't do it, nobody else could have done it. So it follows that nobody could have poisoned the grapefruit."

This was the wrong approach.

"No," said Masters. "And nobody could have exchanged the daggers either. But somebody smacking well *did*."

He extended the palm of his left hand, and with dangerous quietness tapped the forefinger of his right hand in it.

"Don't you see it's the same mess all over again? By our evidence, the only person who could have exchanged the daggers was Mrs. Fane. But she didn't do

150

it, because she had the strongest motive not to. The only person who could have poisoned the grapefruit was Captain Sharpless. But *he* didn't do it, because he had the strongest motive not to. Oh, lummy, lead me to a lunatic asylum."

Black clouds, edged with tarnished silver, shielded a sun which was still brilliant.

H.M. shook his head in slow and sour disbelief. He went over to inspect the dustbin, taking off the lid and replacing it with a clang. Then he pushed open the door of the garden shed, and thrust his big bald head inside. He disclosed nothing more than a lawn-mower, various rakes and shears, a short ladder, a wheelbarrow, and some beach-chairs.

"No!" he said.

"What do you mean, no?" Masters persisted.

"I mean it's not just the blinkin' awful cussedness of things in general. Not this time. It's design."

A step stirred in the gravel path through the rose-garden. Hubert Fane, wearing a gray double-breasted suit, a decorous black tie, and a white rose in his buttonhole, emerged from the garden. The sunlight made his thin hair look like spun glass, and accentuated the slight hollows of his temples. Even his big nose had an air of serenity and benevolence. He carried a pair of shears.

"Good afternoon, my dear," he said, smiling paternally on Ann. "And to you, gentlemen. Chief Inspector Masters I know, but I have not yet had the pleasure of meeting, at least formally, Sir Henry Merrivale."

"How-de-do," said H.M. vaguely. "Been gardenin'?"

"If I have an amiable weakness," replied Hubert, dropping the shears on the ground and dusting his hands with a silk handkerchief, "it is for roses. Like Sergeant Cuff and Cleek and other worthies of detective instincts, I—"

"Know anything about grapefruit?"

Hubert stopped short.

"Not as a gardener. My only knowledge of grapefruit consists of the fact that I cordially dislike it, though my niece is fond of it and my nephew also favored it."

"So? Arthur Fane liked grapefruit too?"

"Yes. Why do you ask?"

"Mrs. Fane took poison in grapefruit," said H.M.

It was seldom possible to surprise Hubert. This almost did it. He remained motionless, a half-smile still on his face.

"Let me be quite clear about this," he requested, after a pause. "Are you attempting to tell me that my courageous but long-suffering niece was poisoned *twice?*"

"No. Only once. There was about three grains of strychnine in the grapefruit that Captain Sharpless carried up to her on Thursday afternoon."

Hubert passed a hand over his smooth hair.

"Now there, my dear sir, permit me to point out that you are talking nonsense."

"No nonsense about it. It's true. Witnesses: one stomach-pump, Dr. Nithsdale, one hospital orderly, me. Were you in the house when Sharpless took the grapefruit up to Mrs. Fane?"

"I was. I remember passing him in the hall. But—"

"Oh? Did you have any conversation with him?"

"Yes. The conversation was as follows. As I passed him I said, 'Grapefruit, eh?' To which he replied, 'Grapefruit,' and went on. Our conversation was distinguished neither for length nor for brilliance of repartee."

"O tempora!" said H.M. "O mores! O hell!"

"Cicero," observed Hubert, "would seem, in this instance, less to the point than the Roman Sybil. Sir, you worry me. What *is* all this?"

H.M. was paying no attention. He was blinking owlishly at the rose-garden. The trellises supporting many of the roses were narrow, of very light wood, in diamond-shaped sections set one above the other, and painted white. Passing from his dour mood, H.M. regarded them with fascination.

"I suppose," volunteered Hubert, "you have come to have some conversations with Victoria?"

"That's the general idea, yes."

"I feel a great interest, very naturally, in her welfare. The dear girl has kindly offered to let me stay on here until I can find a little place of my own. May I earnestly beg you not to worry or distress her with too many questions? She should not, in my opinion, be allowed to see anyone yet."

"I agree with that, Sir Henry," said Ann quickly. "She's trying to do too much at once, and we don't want her to have a relapse. Please! You won't upset her, will you?"

"Oh, we'll be careful. It's only routine stuff, d'ye see, until she gets better." He inflated his chest. "Come along, Masters. We better get this over with." He peered at Courtney and Ann. "You want to come?"

"No, thanks," the former replied with some fervency.

H.M. and Masters had just stumped into the house, with Hubert following them, and Ann had turned to Courtney with a face fierce in desperation, when they had another interruption.

Courtney was shocked at the change in Dr. Richard Rich's appearance. Dr. Rich hurried round the side of the house, round the concrete path past the back drawing-room windows.

His face was haggard. The roll of hair, sprawling out from under the back of his soft black hat, had not been brushed in several days. But the expression on his face was one of relief so great that it might be difficult to express.

"I beg your pardon," said Rich, stopping short and lifting his hat. "Is Sir Henry Merrivale here? The maid said he was 'out back.'"

"He's here, but I don't think you can see him now. They've gone up to speak to Mrs. Fane. Was it anything in particular?"

"I just want to thank him," Rich said simply.

He mopped his forehead.

"He did me the courtesy," Rich went on, "of sending a note round to my lodging house. We don't boast a telephone there. He said that Mrs. Fane's illness was not caused by tetanus, but by strychnine poisoning. He added—"

Rich paused. Fumbling in the breast pocket of his jacket, he drew out a folded sheet of notepaper.

"'There's something else,'" he read aloud, blinking against the sunlight. "'I've got a bit of influence here and there, son. I'd like to reopen your other case—you know what I mean—before the Medical Council. I think we might get you reinstated yet. Chirrup, son. You're not dead yet.'"

Abruptly Rich folded up the letter and put it back in his pocket.

'I never thought I should live to say 'thank God' again," he added, "but I do now."

Ann was standing uncomfortably, her eyes on the ground.

"I'm afraid I said some rather unpleasant things to you the other night, Dr. Rich," she told him. "But I was upset at the time. I'm sorry."

Rich smiled.

"Miss Browning! Lord! That doesn't matter at all. Please forget it. We were all upset, if it comes to that." He smiled again. "You're looking at my hand? It's nothing. I've been very disturbed since Thursday night, and I cut it shaving. A bit of sticking-plaster covers the damage." He brushed this aside. "No. What does matter is this new aspect of the case."

"The strychnine?" said Courtney.

"Yes! The strychnine! Is there some place where we can sit down?"

Courtney led the way along the gravel path through the garden, to the tree-shaded lawn at the back. Ann sat down on the stone bench under the apple tree. Rich, out of condition, panted a little as he perched himself on the opposite end.

"If I'm not too inquisitive," said Ann, "what did that note mean when it said, 'your other case'? What other case?"

Rich's eyes narrowed.

"But you . . . gad, no!" He stared at the past. "You weren't in the room when I told about it. You didn't come in until afterwards. I forgot." Color made his face more red. "It is nothing. Shall we change the subject?"

"What other case? Please!"

Rich contemplated her for a moment.

"Very well," he agreed grimly. "You ought to know with whom you've been breaking bread. I'm a miserable sinner, Miss Browning. I was struck off the medical—"

"Easy, now!" Courtney interposed soothingly. "Is there any necessity for this?"

Rich gestured him to silence.

"—register. I was accused of having . . . if you want to use a polite word, you can say 'seduced' . . . one of my patients while she was under hypnosis."

"Oh."

"I was not guilty. I swear it. One day, perhaps soon, I may be able to prove it. And then! My name will still be mud, of course, so far as general practice is concerned. But some official post: a ship's doctor, say!"

Ann was looking at the branches of the tree overhead. She nodded as though she followed this.

"But to have been accused of this affair, of being mad enough to drive a contaminated pin into a person's arm, would have finished me past all hope. Relieved? Gad, I could dance the fandango!"

"Doctor," said Courtney quietly, "would you mind if *I* asked you one question?"

"Not at all. Ask away."

He filled his pipe, lighted it, and watched the gray smoke hang heavily in the thick thundery air.

Birds bickered among the vines. The stone wall giving on the lane was gray and blotched. These trees, with the green and yellow apples and the dark blue sheen of plums, seemed to shed heat down like the inside of a tent. You could hear the dim hum of wasps.

"Doctor," pursued Courtney, taking the pipe out of his mouth, "on the night you gave that demonstration with the pin, I was outside on the balcony."

Silence.

"You were . . . *what?*"

"I was eavesdropping. Not of my own free will; but there you are. I saw and heard everything you did. In particular, I overheard the questions you asked Mrs. Fane when she was still under hypnosis."

"Indeed," said Rich. His throat seemed dry. His fingers closed round the edges of the bench under him.

"And I heard her answers. What I want to know is why you didn't tell the police about it. H.M. gave you an opportunity to, at that same interview you were speaking of a minute ago. But you said you had nothing to add."

Again silence.

"Do the police," asked Rich, after reflection, "know about this?"

"Yes."

"So it's only a question of time before they—?"

"Ask you? Yes. I wonder they haven't asked you already."

Ann too, he noticed, was watching Rich. But he saw her only out of the tail of his eye. The hum of the quiet, shut-in garden lay drowsy on the senses.

Rich cleared his throat.

"Young man," he said, "this whole affair has consisted in putting me, and me alone, in a series of false positions. You're quite right. I don't deny it. I did ask Mrs. Fane those questions."

"Thanks."

"No sarcasm, sir. I asked the questions because I was curious. Nothing more. I naturally guessed, when I was putting Mrs. Fane through the 'routine' downstairs beforehand, that she had some intense emotional associations with the sofa, that song, and the rest of it. My curiosity was—scientific. I wanted to know who and what and why."

"That's understandable."

"Yes. But wait." Again Rich hesitated. "Well, here's trouble again! But it's got to be told sooner or later. When I asked Mrs. Fane those questions in the bedroom, I heard a certain name."

"Yes. I remember the expression on your face, and how you clenched your fists when you heard it."

Rich closed his eyes, and opened them again.

"Mr. Courtney, a year or two ago, when I was on the stage with my hypnotic turn, I had a girl-assistant. When I talked with Sir Henry Merrivale (again at that same interview), I was off guard: I made a slip of speech; and I almost mentioned that young lady's name."

Courtney nodded.

"Yes," he said. "The girl's name was Polly Allen, wasn't it?"

Sixteen

Rich's face was hot and bitter.

"And I daresay the police know that too?"

"No. At least, not yet. Though they're bound to find it out if they inquire at the theatrical agencies. I only guessed it because I kept thinking of your expression; and that Polly Allen was on the stage, but wouldn't say in what. I'd been thinking a good deal about that girl, because of her resemblance to . . ."

He stopped.

Ann, her chin lifted, had fastened troubled and puzzled eyes on him.

"Yes, you're quite right," admitted Rich, turning out his wrist. "Polly was the girl. You see my position, don't you?"

"I think so. You were afraid that if you told the police they might suspect you had . . ."

"Executed vengeance on Mr. Fane. Exactly."

"You hadn't, had you?"

Rich laughed shortly, a snap of a laugh.

"I had not. I wasn't fond enough of Polly for that. Again, don't misunderstand the position." He made the face of a man always caught by the same misunderstanding. "I wasn't—interested in Polly. In her private life, that is. Polly liked her friends young, I believe. She would have laughed at anybody over forty.

"I could not even be sure it was the same girl. But I knew Polly had disappeared in the middle of July, leaving all her things behind. It was a shock. It was a damned shock. So I decided to keep my mouth shut."

"Again, easily understandable."

"Thank you. I hope the police think so. But I hope they don't think that, even if I had known Arthur Fane killed Polly (which I didn't), I should have got back at him by getting him stabbed. I should simply have gone to the police."

Rich shook his head. He stared at the grass ahead of him. Despite himself, a vein of cynical amusement seemed to well up inside him as he reflected, and his eye twinkled. He was a misunderstood John Bull.

"Lord," he added, "the number of women I *haven't* seduced!"

Courtney laughed. It was the breaking of a tension. He felt again his old liking and respect of Dr. Rich.

"Well," said Rich, slapping his knees and getting up, "I suppose I'd better go in and confess. The longer I keep this thing on my conscience, the worse I shall sleep at night."

"But for your private ear, Doctor: between ourselves, I don't think you've got much to worry about."

Rich stopped.

"No? What makes you think that?"

"You might look at the facts, for one thing. You weren't anywhere near this house on Thursday, were you? That is, until late Thursday night?"

"No, I certainly wasn't. Oh, ah! I see. The strychnine!" Enlightened, Rich rubbed his chin. "In the midst of my own troubles, I almost forgot it. Sir Henry's note said they thought it had been put into a grapefruit."

"That's right. So, unless you can think of a way of

administering strychnine at long range, you can't be counted in. Any more than Miss Browning here can."

Ann was amused.

"Don't be too sure," she mocked him. "*I* was here, you know."

"You were not. You were sitting at Major Adams's with H.M. and Masters and me."

"Oh, not at any of the critical times, I admit. And I certainly never went near that kitchen, even if I did have any earthly reason for wanting to hurt poor Vicky. But I did drop in here to see her about two o'clock, on my way to the major's." The amused shining of her eyes hid a deeper worry she tried to conceal. "So you can put on that as much sinister emphasis as you like."

"Which," said Courtney, "is not much."

"No," smiled Rich. "And as for me, I feel like a free man again." He seemed surprised and a little incredulous, passing a hand across his forehead. "A free man. Released! When I see Merrivale again—"

He had not long to wait in seeing H.M. H.M., in fact, was coming up the path at that moment. With his baggy sports-coat flapping above white flannels, he seemed distraught and in something of a hurry.

Rich's face lit up.

"Sir Henry," he began, "I want to thank—"

H.M.'s manner was fussed and fussy.

"That's all right, son." He waved his hand. "Some other time. Oh, I say: wait. Masters wants a word with you. He's down in the kitchen now, givin' the cook hysterics. Go and see him, will you?"

"With pleasure!" declared Rich, and marched away as though to music.

Though H.M. tried to smooth out the expression of his face, Courtney could see that something was up. He felt a quiver of what might have been apprehension. Against the heat of the day H.M. mopped his forehead with a handkerchief, and took off his spectacles and polished them, before fitting them back on like a war-helmet.

"You," he said to Ann. "Go in and see Mrs. Fane. She wants to talk to you." He looked at Courtney. "You better go too. No, burn it, you're not intrudin'! She especially asked to see you."

The uneasiness increased.

"But what's up, sir?"

"Never you mind what's up. Just do as I say. Mrs. Fane'll tell you. Don't go through the kitchen: there's merry blazes goin' on there. Go round the side of the house and in at the front. Go on. Shoo!"

Laboriously H.M. lowered himself to the bench. He had the air of one who wants to be alone. Taking another of the black, oily cigars out of his pocket, he lit it and blew out a vast volume of smoke.

In their last sight of him, as Courtney knocked out his pipe and followed Ann down the path, he was sitting under the thick-branching apple tree, his spectacles down on his nose, the cigar in one corner of his mouth, staring with evil-faced absorption at his own shoes.

They circled the house, and went in. The upstairs hall was sun-filled, warm, and deserted. Ann tapped at the front bedroom door.

"Come in," said an attractive voice.

It seemed to Courtney years since he had seen that bedroom. Nothing was changed, except that all trace of Arthur had been tidied away or removed.

There was the light maplewood bed, with the golden tan quilted coverlet. The round mirror of the dressing table on the far side. The bedside lamp with its mirror base. The writing-desk between the windows. The long windows to the balcony, now standing open.

In the bed Vicky Fane was propped up against pillows, from where she could look straight across to the windows and out over the trees in the avenue.

She was handsomer than Courtney remembered her, for her face now had life and animation. She turned her head, with difficulty, to greet them; the jaws and neck were still tender and somewhat swollen, though this hardly showed. The tan partly concealed her pallor. She was wearing a lace negligee over her nightgown.

Vicky smiled at them, also with difficulty, showing fine teeth.

"Do come in," she requested. Her voice was faintly husky, "This room's a sight, I'm afraid. But we let the nurse go; I'm perfectly fit. I could play six sets of tennis now and never feel it."

"You know you couldn't," said Ann rather sharply.

Vicky ignored this.

"You're Mr. Courtney, aren't you?"

"Yes, Mrs. Fane. I don't like to barge in like this—"

" 'Vicky,' please, And you're not barging in." She gave him her hand, and he took it. "You're a great friend of Frank's, aren't you? He's told me so much about you."

A vast inner happiness seemed to sustain her and glow through her. This, and her will-power. For he could see that she was still very ill, and that she got round this by refusing to admit it.

He did not quite know what to say. If he said, "I've heard about you and Frank; many congratulations," that would hardly do. But if he said, "I'm sorry to hear of the death of your husband," that would be worse. So he said nothing, while Vicky dreamed.

"I understand," she went on, rousing herself and smiling, "that I gave all of you rather a bad time on Thursday night."

"Not at all."

"No, certainly not," agreed Ann, rearranging the coverlet. "And please stop thinking about it!"

"My dear, somebody's got to think about it," Vicky

said practically. "We may as well admit that we're in an awful mess, and that I came luckily out of it."

He wondered if she knew what had been really wrong with her. Evidently not.

Her eyes were somber. "But I wonder," Vicky said, touching her throat gingerly, "I wonder, Ann, whether you'd do me a great favor?"

"Of course."

"I wonder whether you would come and stay here with me tonight? And maybe tomorrow night too? Chief Inspector Masters says he can arrange it with Colonel Race, if you have to be away."

Outside the windows, dim and far off, there was a very faint flicker of lightning.

Ann stood with her hands on the foot of the bed, motionless.

"Of course I will!" She opened her lips, hesitated, and then dared it. "But you don't think there's any— any—"

Vicky attempted to laugh; but this was clearly painful, for she gave it up.

"No, no, no!" she assured them both. "Nothing like that. But, it's just that I want—company. And I can hardly have Mrs. Propper or Daisy."

She lowered her eyes and plucked at the coverlet.

"You see, Ann, after all I *am* a murderess."

"Vicky!"

"My dear, it's perfectly true. I'm not going to get hysterical, or try to keep thinking about it. But I did kill poor Arthur, even if I didn't know what I was doing. You can't deny that, can you?"

"No; but you weren't to blame, any more than the dagger itself was to blame. You were just a—a—"

"A thing," Vicky finished for her. "A thing that walked and talked and moved and did what it was told. But, do you know, I hate being a 'thing.' I did kill Arthur. I even had his heart marked for me, with a cross drawn in pencil, so I couldn't miss it. At least, that's what they tell me. 'X marks the spot!' That's what's happened through this whole thing. All drawn and diagrammed for somebody else."

Ann spoke quietly.

"Vicky, what have the police been saying to you?"

"Nothing. That is—nothing. They haven't upset me, if that's what you mean. They were terribly nice, really. And Sir Henry Merrivale lives up to all I'd ever heard."

Ann walked round the bed and half leaned, half sat on the edge of the dressing table. Her cheeks were flushed, her eyes troubled.

"Vicky, I—I hadn't meant to ask you. Even when I was up here before, I've kept and kept myself from asking you. But how much do you remember?"

There was a silence.

"Not very much. I remember Dr. Rich talking to me, and that coin shining. The next thing I distinctly remember is waking up on the bed here, and feeling horribly tired and shaky, with Frank's arm round me.

"I said, 'For heaven's sake, don't; suppose Arthur should see?' Then he had to tell me."

"Stop, Vicky! That's enough!"

"No. It's all right. I don't mind. But in between, you see, it's all darkness and noises. I'll tell you what it's like. Did you ever go on a binge? And have too much to drink? And then wake up again next morning, without an earthly notion of what you'd been doing; and feeling ghastly and thinking of all the dreadful things you *might* have done?"

Ann nodded guiltily.

"Not that I go on binges, much," explained Vicky, turning her candid dark-blue eyes towards Courtney, and smiling, "but I do remember one at New Year's, when Arthur and I were first married. I don't think he ever forgave me. His suits are still over in that wardrobe. Get me some water, will you? It hurts to swallow; but my throat's so dry I've just got to have it."

Ann poured out a quarter of a tumbler of water from the carafe on the bedside-table. Holding the glass in both hands, Vicky drank. She was fighting with all the vigor of her nature to keep herself steady.

"Don't ever be hypnotized, Ann," she advised, handing the glass back. "At least, if you're made to do what I was. It's not nice."

"And what are you going to do now?"

"I'm going to marry Frank," answered Vicky, with flat candor. "That is, if I think it won't hurt his career. But if there's scandal, and I think it will hurt his career, I'm going to take a place near where he's stationed, and live with him.... Does that seem very dreadful to you, Phil Courtney?"

He returned her smile.

"Not at all. But I think you'd both be happier married. There's no objection to the other thing, except that it so seldom works out."

Vicky clenched her fists.

"If we could only—" She lowered her voice. "If we could only find the beast who's doing this! The person behind it.... The cruel, clever beast who made me kill Arthur, and then tried to get rid of me with what they say is the most painful poison there is. That's what I can't forgive. The *pain*."

"So the police did tell you, then," breathed Ann.

"Well . . . yes. And I thought that grapefruit tasted funny at the time anyway."

"You're sure it *was* in the grapefruit?"

"Yes. They didn't suggest it to me. I suggested it to them; the police, I mean. You see, I kept the spoon."

"Kept the spoon?"

"Yes. Accidentally. The spoon that came with the grapefruit. It was left behind when Daisy took the tray down. I saw it a minute or two later, and put it on the dressing table over there, meaning to give it to Daisy when she brought the tea up. Only I began to feel horrible in the meantime, so I forgot it. It's been there all the time. I gave it to Inspector Masters just now. He says if there are traces of strychnine on it—"

Courtney did not ask her if she knew who had carried the grapefruit up. Or, to be more exact, if she knew who was the only person who could have poisoned it.

And, undoubtedly, neither H.M. nor Masters had told her.

"You're exciting yourself, Vicky," said Ann, "and you've got to stop. Please. Lie back. There's a good girl."

Vicky relaxed.

"Yes," admitted Vicky wryly. "I was told not to talk too much. By the doctor, I mean. But you will come and stay the night, won't you, Ann?"

"Of course I will. I'll go over and pack a bag and come back now."

"I'd appreciate it awfully if you would. There's nothing to be afraid of, you understand. It's just that I want company. And I have—dreams."

"I understand. Come along, Phil."

Psychic fits again?

Once more faint lightning flickered in the west. The oppressiveness of the day, the heat of the day, the moods of the day, may have produced the feeling. As he said good-by to Vicky, he felt not for the only time that sensation of evil which he had first experienced when he stood on the balcony outside these windows. Now it was coming closer. And it was growing stronger.

He was afterwards to remember this scene, with Vicky's cool hand in his, and the old-rose curtains writhing slightly as a breeze gathered, and the almost imperceptible darkening of the room. That flicker beyond the windows caught Vicky's eye.

"Heat-lightning," she said.

"Yes," said Ann. "Heat-lightning. Phil, come *on*."

Seventeen

The rain poured down.

"Then we're all agreed," said Sir Henry Merrivale, "that there's only one person who can be guilty?"

In Inspector Agnew's office at the police station, Agnew, H.M., and Masters had their chairs drawn up to the inspector's roll-top desk. On this desk, under the light, lay small groups of articles and official forms. Latest to be added to them was a small spoon, together with the analyst's report that in the coating of grapefruit juice adhering to the spoon he had found one-fifteenth of a grain of $C_{21}H_{22}N_2O_2$, or strychnine.

Rain sluiced down the windows and gurgled along the gutters. It was nearly ten o'clock.

"We're agreed on that?" demanded H.M.

"Definitely," said Agnew.

"Oh, ah," conceded Masters, cautious even here.

"Good. Then what in the name of St. Ignatius's beans is delayin' you? Write out your warrant and get the chief constable to sign it. There's no honey-sweet savor about these murders. I tell you, our friend is too dangerous to be allowed loose any longer."

Masters fingered his chin.

"We're protecting that gal," pursued H.M., "as

168

much as we can, without actually havin' a policeman sleeping with her—"

"Now, now!" growled Masters, his sense of the proprieties offended.

"But we can't go on doin' it forever. Something's got to be done, and done quick."

Inspector Agnew picked up the spoon and tapped it on the desk.

"Do you think, sir," he asked, "that the person in question has twigged it that we know what we do know?"

H.M. meditated.

"I don't see how, son. The subject's never been brought up, at least by Masters or me; and our star witness is primed in case questions are asked. Now, Masters, speak up: what about it?"

Masters was dogged.

"Now, sir, it's all very well to say that," he complained. "But we can't go flying off the handle like that. I admit that the person you say is guilty *is* guilty. Lummy, I can't very well deny it! We've been fooled by as innocent-faced a piece of acting from a thoroughgoing snake as I ever saw."

"You're right there," agreed Agnew, contemplating the past without amusement.

"Very well!" said Masters. "The case is good. But it's not complete."

He tapped a sheaf of documents.

"We've got here evidence of motive: that's good. We've got here," he tapped an official form, "the statement of the chemist, Lewis L. Lewis: that's better. We've got here, after some downright fine staff-work by Inspector Agnew," continued Masters, who believes in keeping in well with the local police, "evidence of the purchase of the knife in Gloucester. That's still better."

He held up the knife with which Arthur Fane had

been stabbed. It still bore, at a distance, resemblance to a rubber one.

"The ironmonger's willing to identify the person who bought it. That was a bad bloomer on our friend's part. But it always happens. These clever people *will* do it."

Masters put down the knife, and picked up an official cellophane envelope containing traces of a whitish powder.

"Finding the stuff itself, in the place where we did find it. Lummy! That's the best yet. So far as I'm concerned personally, or a jury's concerned, that's hanging evidence. But, sir, the case isn't complete. It's all very well to say, 'Write out your warrant.' We can't make out one, and the chief constable can't sign it, until we know how the ruddy knife was used, and how the person in question managed to exchange it with the toy one in full view of all the other witnesses."

"Oh, that?" murmured H.M., as though completely uninterested.

Masters pushed his chair away from the desk. His temper was simmering again.

"Oh, that?" he mimicked. "I suppose you don't think that's important?"

"It's important. Sure. But it's not difficult."

"No? You just tell me how it was done—tell me a practical way—and I'll have our friend in chokey before you can say Jack Robinson. The poison-in-the-grapefruit part of the thing, I admit, is easy. That's just what we thought it must be. But the dagger business has got me up a tree, and I don't mind saying so."

H.M. looked distressed.

"Oh, son, think! I thought you'd tumbled to it long ago. Especially considering what went on in that room that you've heard all about but haven't understood. And considering that most people's idea of usin' their eyesight and estimatin' time is rummy enough to interest J.W. Dunne."

The rain sluiced down. H.M. was an hour and ten minutes late. Courtney, having brought no raincoat to Cheltenham, had been imperfectly protected on the journey out by an umbrella he borrowed from the hall-porter at The Plough. His shoes and trouser-legs were soaking. Worse than this were the twinges of disquiet he experienced as the hour grew later.

"Rather odd experience, what?" inquired the major, comfortably pulling at a cheroot. "I'll tell you an odder. At Poona, in nineteen-o-nine . . ."

Out in the hall, the telephone rang.

Courtney jumped up.

"That's probably for me," he said. "You don't mind if I answer it?"

"My dear chap!" said the major. "Dammit. Not at all. Do."

When he took down the receiver, a female voice spoke. It spoke in a quick, stealthy whisper, shaking with terror so that the words were barely distinguishable.

"I want to speak to the doctor."

"Wrong number," said Courtney wearily. "What number did you want?"

The voice grew softly frenzied. "I want double-four, double-four. Isn't that double-four, double-four?"

"Yes, that's right. But there's no doctor here. Doctor who?"

"The big doctor!"

Light broke on him. "You mean Sir Henry Merrivale? Isn't that Mrs. Propper speaking?"

"Yes, yes, yes! (S-s-hh! Daisy, if you carry on like that we'll both get our throats cut!) Oh, my God."

"Mrs. Propper! Listen! This is Courtney here. Mr. Courtney."

"His secretary?"

"Well—yes. What is it? What's wrong?"

The voice grew even softer. "Sir, you've got to come

over here. Somebody's got to come over here. There's a man in the house. A burglar. I saw him climb in through the winder."

Score another for psychic fits!

"Listen, Mrs. Propper. Can you hear me? Right! Go down and wake up Mr. Fane, Mr. Hubert Fane . . ."

"I wouldn't stir out of this room," said the voice passionately, "not if you was to give me all the money in the Bank of England."

"But where are you speaking from?"

"I'm speaking from my bedroom. There's an extension telephone here. Oh, sir, for God's sake send the big doctor over here. Or come yourself. I wouldn't go near them nasty police, after what they said to me to-day, not if you was to give me—"

"Right. I'll come straight away. But somebody's got to let me in."

There was a fierce, whispered colloquy with an even more frightened Daisy.

"When you get here," muttered Mrs. Propper, who was gratifyingly quick-witted as a conspirator, "give three rings on the doorbell—one, two, three—so's we'll know it's you. Then we'll run downstairs and let you in."

"Right. Good-by."

The tone of his voice, though he tried to keep it casual, was such as to bring Major Adams popping out of the library.

"Anything up, old chap?"

"That was the Fanes' cook. There's a burglar in the house. I'm going over there now."

The major's eyes gleamed.

"Is there, by Jove? Need any help?"

"No, thanks. I can manage."

The major was depressed. But he was sportsman enough to see that this was the other fellow's shot.

"Take a mack from the hatrack. Wait here. Back in half a second. Know just what you want."

He darted upstairs. He returned lovingly carrying a three-thirty express rifle which, at a conservative estimate, would have stopped a charging tiger at five hundred yards.

"Take it along," he said. "Always wondered what one of these things would do to a burglar. Nobody ever burgles this house, dammit. Take it with you. Might be useful. What?"

"*But I can't—*"

"My dear chap, not another word. Rain won't hurt it. Fell in the river with it once myself. If you don't feel up to potting the blighter, you can use it to intimidate him with. Or I can get you a pair of knuckle-dusters, if you'd rather? Might be useful. What?"

He was already bustling Courtney into a mackintosh. The raincoat, several sizes too small, set Courtney's wrists some inches out of the sleeves and threatened to crack across the shoulders.

"What I mean is, I can't go about firing rifles at burglars in other people's houses! In the first place, it's illegal. In the second place, if I used this thing on him they'd have to scrape him off the walls. In the third place—"

"Here's your hat," said the major, jamming it down on his head. "Better hurry. Good hunting, my dear chap. If I hear any rumpus I'll come and lend a hand."

The door closed, and he was shut out in the rain.

He set out at a run. But the path was slippery, the gate greasy, the pavement of Fitzherbert Avenue like a water-chute. He had to slow down, or he would have gone head over ears.

It was a tropical rain which must have made many of the residents feel at home. There was no thunder or lightning; only a steady driving deluge which struck the pavement to rebound up again under your chin, and in which you could not even have heard yourself shout.

Even the street-lamps were hardly visible. Courtney put his head down and butted along against the downpour. He could feel his hat and collar growing sodden, and the heavy squelch of his shoes. But the thought which crowded out all others in this roaring gloom was that Mrs. Propper's intruder was not a burglar of the sort she thought—and that Ann Browning, alone except for an equally terrified Vicky Fane, was shut up in a room which already held enough unpleasant memories.

His skin felt clammy. He was glad he had the rifle, now.

When he reached the gate, he was running again. Beyond the front lawn, "The Nest" showed dim and whitish through the sheen of rain. And there was no light in the house.

He ran up the path, feeling the breath rasp in his lungs. Whatever this "burglar" might be doing, he would hardly continue it if he heard somebody at the door. Courtney glanced up at the windows of Vicky's bedroom. They were dark, but they might only be curtained.

With a deep wave of thankfulness he pounded up the front steps.

He gave Mrs. Propper's signal, three short rings at the doorbell, and waited.

Nothing stirred in the house. He could hear only the rustling roar of the rain, the rush from a water-spout, the drumming on his own body. The minutes dragged by, and still nothing happened. In desperation, he again gave the signal of three sharp rings, before he realized where the trouble lay.

The doorbell did not work.

Eighteen

He stood back and studied the house.

No doubt about the bell being out of order. It had a distinctive ring which could be heard clearly in the hall and outside.

And a "burglar" who puts bells out of order—

He tried the front door, but it was locked. The proper thing to attract attention, according to accepted canons, was to throw a handful of gravel against a window. But he saw no gravel. And since Mrs. Propper, he remembered, slept on the top floor of the house, the chances of scoring an audible hit with a handful of gravel in the rain were remote even if he had known which room she slept in.

At the foot of the front steps he found half a brick. Weighing this in his hand, he considered. People like H.M. or Major Adams might announce their arrival at somebody's house by chucking half a brick through a pane of glass, but its effect on frightened women might be worse than that of the burglar.

If he could attract the attention of Ann or Vicky, though—

And there was a gravel path through the rose-garden, at the back of the house.

He tried shouting at the window, but even the effects

of powerful lungs were smothered and lost in the downpour. At least, there was no reply.

When he hurried round to get the gravel, his mind was divided between blind panic and a sense of the ridiculousness of the position. Here was he, a great gawk carrying an express rifle, outside a house and unable to get in. There might, even, be nothing wrong. Both Mrs. Propper and Daisy were in a state to see burglars where no burglars existed.

And, come to think of it, how had this burglar got in? Through a window, Mrs. Propper had said. But all the ground-floor windows were well up from the ground. . . .

Human life seldom gives us the opportunity to be wholly unself-conscious or wholly heroic. Smashing windows with bricks, when a very ill woman lies upstairs, and the result may merely meet with a certain impatience on the part of those inside: no. They did these things in the films. They did them in the stories. But, when you faced such situation in real life, you only ran in circles.

Scooping up a handful of gravel from the path behind the house, Courtney saw, dimly looming, the outline of the garden shed. It gave him another idea. There was, he remembered from this afternoon, a ladder in the shed.

And if the burglar could get in through a window, supposing there to be a burglar, why couldn't he?

Despite the mackintosh, his clothes now felt like a weight of cold, wet pulp; his hat hung sodden over a streaming pair of eyes. He groped forward towards the shed. His wet fingers had some difficulty with the catch of the door. Inside, in a close mustiness with the rain hammering on the roof, he stepped on a rake and blundered into the lawn-mower (a whole welter of inanimate objects endowed with whirring, malicious noise) before he struck a match.

The ladder, as he remembered from this afternoon, was a short ladder. It would reach one of the ground-floor windows. He trundled it out, bringing down with a crash everything which had been stood upright.

Not difficult, though. Propping the ladder against the concrete drive behind the house, he lowered it until its upper edge rested on the sill of the nearer back drawing-room window.

And the window at the top was unlocked. He was just raising it when he remembered that he had left Major Adams's infernal rifle lying on the floor in the shed.

Why bother, anyway?

The rifle was no good to him.

Pushing up the window to the top, writhing round awkwardly like a squeezed concertina until he could sit on the window-sill, he pushed his legs through and dropped into a pitch-black room.

Many times, of course, he had heard described the agonizing cracks and creaks which could be drawn from the floor here. But when those creaks and cracks burst out, suddenly, under his own feet, he nearly jumped out of a crawling skin.

Disentangling himself from the curtains, he stood upright and listened. No noise, no life, no movement in a dark room. He took a step forward, waking the creaks again. He had never been in this room before. He had no notion of where the light-switch lay, except that it was probably by the door. And the door would be—yes. Ahead a good way, then to the left.

Courtney struck a match.

On the sofa where Polly Allen had been strangled, white and ghostly in that feeble light, someone was sitting and looking at him.

He let the match burn nearly out before he dropped it. The ensuing darkness was worse; for it brought out with vividness, like the pattern of a light after you have turned it off, the scattered details he could place of that motionless figure.

"Who's there?" he said aloud. "Speak up! *Who's there?*"

The words were hardly out of his mouth before he remembered, as though of an impression hitherto arrested, the flat darkish patch of dried blood from the left temple of the motionless figure down to its cheek.

Courtney got out another match. He managed to strike it, though by this time his wet fingers had half soaked the box. His shoes squelched and slipped on the hardwood as, carrying the match cradled like a sacred flame, shoulders humped, not daring to look round, he walked across towards the door in search of light.

There were three light-switches beside the door. He pressed the top one, and nothing happened. He pressed the one below, and the white glow of a lamp in a parchment shade—a bridge lamp—sprang up beside the white arm of the sofa.

That sofa had been pushed a little way out into the room, the lamp set beside it so that someone sitting and reading on the sofa would get a good light over the left shoulder. And the thick upholstery had prevented the body from sliding down farther than the line of its shoulders, where the coat had rucked up at the back.

Hubert Fane, barely alive from concussion of the brain, sat as though sprawled at ease. His left arm rested on the arm of the sofa. An open copy of the *Tatler* lay across his lap.

The neatness of his dinner jacket and linen, the careful way in which the trousers had been plucked up to avoid bagging at the knees, above black silk socks and brightly polished shoes: all these things contrasted with the corpselike face and the wound in the back of the skull from which blood had ceased to flow.

Courtney forced himself to walk across. Though every muscle twitched with repulsion, he forced himself to touch Hubert. He rolled back the eyelid, exposing no iris. He touched the back of the head, which felt soft. A thin thread of breath trickled through Hubert's body: no more. The white light of the lamp brought it out clearly, the homelike room with the flowers on the grand piano, and Hubert, who had been sitting reading the *Tatler* when someone he knew opened the door. . . .

Easy to get behind a person. Then leave the room quietly, turning out the light.

Upstairs.

What was happening upstairs?

Phil Courtney has since thought that his first sight of that dummy figure, sitting as though so quietly and comfortably in the dark, had numbed his wits to such an extent that he did not move until the thought of Ann, upstairs, occurred to him.

Outside the rain splashed and drummed.

Courtney ran for the door. He slipped on one of the treacherous rugs, and saved himself only by banging into the wall. This room was infected. He wanted to get out of it.

The light from this drawing room flung a bright path into the hall. It showed him the staircase. Groping, he found the handrail and took the stairs three steps at a time.

The upstairs hall was dark too, but a line of light lay under the sill of the door to Vicky Fane's bedroom.

At any other time, the idea of throwing open a bedroom door at this time of night without even so much as knocking would have seemed beyond the limits of possible behavior. But, after turning the knob and finding that it was not locked, he went in.

The bedside lamp was on, shining down over the busy clock. Vicky Fane, the tan coverlet drawn up to her breast, lay asleep—or evidently asleep—on the far side. Two pillows were under her head, and her arms from the sleeveless white nightgown lay outside the coverlet. She breathed deeply but sometimes with a sob or jerk, which made her tremble.

Ann Browning, wearing a flowered dressing robe over gray silk pajamas, stood at the other side of the bed, half bending over Vicky.

In her right hand Ann held a small hypodermic syringe with a polished metal barrel and long, pinlike needle.

Ann looked up at him across the width of the bed. Her eyes widened, and her mouth fell open.

"Phil Courtney," she said, "what on earth are you doing here?"

"Not you," he said. "Oh, my God, not *you?*"

He does not remember saying this, though it has often been quoted against him since.

What he does remember is every detail of the room: colors, outlines, even the fall of shadows. The gleam of the sharp needle. The glass water-carafe, and a little round box of white tablets, among bottles on the bedside table. The druggy medicinal smell of the room, since the windows were closed. The hypnotic drive of the rain. The vague, pinching shadow, the movement of the lips and muscles as at pain stirring again, which had begun to creep across the face of the unconscious Vicky Fane.

Pain . . .

Most of all, he remembered Ann's frightened, horrified face as she looked back at him.

"You don't think," she cried, "that *I*—?" She flung the needle from her, clumsily. It landed on the coverlet and rolled.

Several buckets of water poured over Phil Courtney could have made him no wetter than he was. Yet the sensation of a bucket of water flung in the face, the drop of anti-climax after the grotesque thought that had occurred to him, partly restored sane values. If they were not altogether restored, it was because Vicky Fane moaned.

"What's going on here?" he said. "Do you know there's supposed to be a burglar in the house?"

"I—burglar? How do you know?"

"Mrs. Propper phoned over to the major's. Didn't you hear me yelling outside?"

"N-no. Was it you who made that noise?"

"What noise?"

"A-about twenty minutes ago. When Vicky'd taken her sleeping-tablets and gone to sleep, and I was t-trying to. I was frightened out of my wits. It was a noise like something heavy falling. Downstairs. I w-went down to look, but I was frightened and I ran back up again."

"Go on. Anything else?"

Ann had her hands pressed flat to her fiery cheeks. Her eyes regarded him with incredulous horror. Her mind was evidently obsessed with only one thing.

"You," she said slowly, "thought that *I* . . ."

"I don't know what I thought, so help me! Hubert Fane's downstairs now with the back of his head bashed in. There's something going on. Wait! I'm sorry I said that! He may not be badly hurt. I—"

She caught at the footboard of the bed to keep herself from falling. But she pointed to the hypodermic.

"I—I came back up here. I knew I couldn't sleep. I just walked about. Finally I decided to take one of Vicky's sleeping-tablets. I came over here," she illustrated by turning towards the bedside table, "and I was going to pick up the box, when I saw that syringe-thing on the table. I hadn't noticed it there before. Maybe it's something the doctors give Vicky. It must be! You don't think—?"

"How long were you out of the room?"

"About two minutes."

Twenty minutes ago. Twenty minutes ago. Twenty

minutes ago. Vicky's lips twitched. The clock ticked loudly.

Courtney went across to the bed. His mackintosh and shoes were soaking the carpet, but he paid no attention. He picked up the hypodermic needle. Fishing in his pocket after a handkerchief, he pressed the plunger of the needle gently. He had pressed it entirely down before a drop of water, or what looked like clear water, touched the fabric.

Gingerly he touched his tongue to it. Even in an alcohol solution and in such small quantity, the intensely bitter sting of it burnt his tongue. He swabbed out his mouth with haste and fierceness.

"Strychnine again," he said.

"Are you sure?"

"I'm no doctor. But you can't very well mistake this stuff. If it is strychnine, injected straight into the bloodstream with a hypodermic, they may not be able to save her this time. Steady, now!"

A violent shudder, as though it were she herself who felt the symptoms, went through Ann's body. Time seemed to rush on while they tried to arrest it.

"I'm all right," she said steadily, and drew the dressing robe closer about her with a hard, bright look in her eyes. "What do we do?"

"Do you know Dr. Nithsdale's telephone number?"

"Nine-seven-o-one. He's our doctor."

"I'll go down and phone him. You run up and rout out Mrs. Propper and Daisy. Tell them to prepare . . . no, blast it, an emetic's no good if the poison wasn't taken through the mouth!" His head was whirling. "I wish to heaven I knew what to do in the meantime. I don't know *what* we ought to do. Anyway, rout them out. Hurry!"

"I'll do it," said Ann calmly. "And I'll never speak to you again as long as I live."

There was no time to argue over this. Muttering

"nine-seven-o-one, nine-seven-o-one," convinced that he would forget it by the time he reached the phone, he raced downstairs.

Where was the telephone anyway? Stop they always spoke of it as being in the back drawing room. He was not anxious to face that gruesome object sitting so comfortably, with the *Tatler* across its lap and the bloodstain down its ear to the collar. But it had to be done.

The telephone was on a little round table by the windows, almost within touching-distance of Hubert. With an unsteady finger Courtney dialed the number and got it right. The ringing-tone buzzed interminably in his head while he perched on the edge of a little chair, staring at the phone. It had rung for a full minute, which to Courtney seemed interminable, before Dr. Nithsdale's voice answered.

When he had explained, Dr. Nithsdale's language was sulphurous.

"And also," Courtney added, "come prepared to deal with somebody who's got a bash over the back of the head, probably—"

"Lad, are you clean daft?"

"No, no, no! There's a lunatic in the house tonight. Just do what I ask. But, Doctor!"

"Aye?"

"If the strychnine was administered with a hypodermic, what can I do about it in the meantime?"

"Naething. And it isna likely *I* can either. Guid-by."

The receiver went up with a bang.

Courtney pressed his hands to a throbbing head. Beside him the rain was spattering in from the open window, so that bright needles stung the floor and drenched the curtains. No other sound disturbed the house.

He swung round to face Hubert, and got what was perhaps his worst shock of the night—at least, so far. Hubert, still in the same position, had not stirred. But his eyes were wide open, and they were looking straight into Courtney's from not six feet away.

"Good evening," Hubert said in an agreeable if slightly furred and wandering voice. "I seem to have fallen asleep. Most extraordinary. Most extraordinary."

Nineteen

Yet it was not Hubert Fane in his right senses. Courtney realized this when he noted the expression of the eyes.

He remembered a friend of his who had suffered concussion of the brain from being struck by the door of a railway carriage. After being knocked out, this friend had got up assuring everyone that nothing was wrong with him, and had gone about his business until he collapsed many hours later.

Hubert, grotesquely neat except for the stain of dried blood down his face, blinked and touched a hand to his forehead.

"Extraordinary," he continued in the same buzzy, benevolent voice. The *Tatler* slid off his knees to the floor. "Do you know I cannot remember—"

"Steady, sir!"

"May I ask, Mr. Courtney, how you came here? And would you do me the esthetic favor of removing that extremely disreputable coat and hat?"

"Look here—"

"My head does indeed feel excessively odd. Not painful, but odd. I surely cannot have taken that much brandy after dinner."

Courtney felt his throat grow dry. "Who," he said, "was last in this room with you, Mr. Fane?"

A look of mild wonder overspread Hubert's face.

"Now there," he replied, running his fingers lightly over his forehead, "is another remarkable thing. I cannot recall how I came here. The last thing I distinctly remember is sitting in the library reading the evening paper. This room has not associations so pleasant that I should sit in it by choice. I think it would soothe me to go and bathe my eyes. Yes, I must go and bathe my eyes."

"Hold on, Mr. Fane!" cried Courtney, as Hubert got to his feet and stood swaying on his spidery legs. "Don't get up! Stay there! You've been hurt."

"I have been what?"

"You've been hurt."

"My dear sir, what nonsense you talk," said Hubert mildly, and went over flat on his face on the floor.

Courtney looked round in desperation, wondering what to do here. He was in time to see another person looking at him.

Through the open window and the blowing curtains, stung with rain, projected the head and shoulders of Sir Henry Merrivale. H.M. was swathed round in a transparent oilskin with a hood, which covered everything including his hat, and was not a sight for weak nerves. Out of this he glared through misted spectacles.

"What's goin' on here?" he demanded. "Who put this ladder up to the window?"

"I did. I had to get in somehow." Courtney could have yelled with relief. "Come on in and tell us what's to be done."

"Oh. I thought . . ." H.M. broke off, and sniffed. He pointed a malignant forefinger. "What's wrong with *him*?"

"You tell me."

Though it was a near thing. H.M. did manage to

squeeze through the window. He flapped among the curtains and almost tore them down from their rods. He landed on the floor with a thud that shook the ceiling. But he did manage to get in. Trailing water and oilskin, he waddled across to the prone figure and bent over it.

"Concussion," he said, after examination. "And a bad one. Lord love a duck!"

"Never mind him," urged Courtney, not very sympathetically for Hubert. "Go upstairs. Mrs. Fane's been attacked again. The murderer gave her another dose of strychnine in a hypodermic, and Dr. Nithsdale says—"

There was more bumping behind him. First Masters, and then Inspector Agnew, pushed through the window and dropped inside. A mist arose as they shook themselves. Bright puddles of rainwater ran and glistened on the hardwood.

"Don't anybody ever answer the door at this place?" questioned an exasperated chief inspector. "We've been hammering at the front door for the past ten minutes. The bell won't work."

"Don't you hear what I'm saying?" shouted Courtney. "It's Mrs. Fane. Strychnine again! I've phoned the doctor. But somebody sneaked in while Ann was out of the room, and gave her a hypodermic full of it. She's in bad shape."

"Is she, now?" said H.M. tonelessly.

It took a little while for this to penetrate into Courtney's mind. It took a little while for him to understand the implications of H.M.'s casual, uninterested tone. And even then he did not understand it.

"H.M., are you crazy? Are you all crazy? Why don't you do something? She must have got the whole hypodermic full of it. When I pressed the handle of the thing, there was only a drop left. I touched it to my tongue, and it was bitter—"

"So," said H.M., peering round over his shoulder out of the dripping oilskin. "You touched it to your tongue, did you?"

"Yes."

"Uh-huh. Did it make the tip of your tongue feel numb afterwards?"

"No."

"Sure of that, son?"

"Yes, quite sure."

"Then," said H.M., turning back again, "it wasn't strychnine."

There was a silence, except for the sluicing rain. Masters and Agnew stood motionless, a stuffed expression on their faces.

Courtney stared at them wildly.

"Would someone," requested a courteous voice from the floor, "would someone be good enough to assist me to my feet? I am quite well, but my—er—motor reflexes appear not to motor in the accepted sense of the term. It is most annoying."

"Agnew!"

"Sir?"

"Get this feller up to his room," said H.M. "He's hurt bad. Come on." As Agnew hurried over, he scowled at Courtney and went on. "I'll have a look at Mrs. Fane, just in case."

"Now then," said Masters, "what's all this? What's been going on, Mr. Courtney?"

When Courtney started to tell him, Masters walked across to the sofa. He went round it, studying. From the floor behind the sofa he picked up a heavy roughstonework jar, whose surface would have held no fingerprints but which must have weighed ten or twelve pounds and would have made a murderous weapon. Masters weighed it in his hand.

Courtney, however, did not waste much time in telling his story. He raced upstairs after H.M.

There was a babble of voices in the upstairs hall. Mrs. Propper and Daisy, muffled up in extra clothing as though they would have to leave a house on fire, were excitedly pouring out to Ann a story which was far from clear.

"Here's the big doctor!" howled Mrs. Propper, clutching at H.M. as he passed. "You go in there, sir. You go and see Mrs. Fane!"

"Now, now, lemme alone! For cat's sake lemme alone. I . . ."

H.M. went into the front bedroom. Stripping off the waterproof, he bent over Vicky Fane. He picked up one limp wrist and took her pulse. He ran his fingers lightly from under the ears down along the line of the jaws, and round the neck. He lifted one eyelid and looked at the iris. Though his manner seemed more malevolent than ever, yet Courtney felt that a shadow had passed from his face, and that he breathed more easily.

"Well?" Courtney demanded. "What is it? What's wrong with her?"

"Nothing."

"*Nothing?*" cried Ann.

They were crowded in the doorway, peering, like a cluster of people in a Hogarth sketch.

"You mean she hasn't had anything at all?"

"Nothing," responded H.M., "except the chloral in her sleeping-tablets. Oh, my eye, what a fine lot of scare-mongers *you* are. Now see here. What's all this rumpus about a burglar? We went down to Adams's place, and he was all hoppin' about sending you—" he blinked at Courtney—"out with a rifle to pot a burglar. What burglar?"

Mrs. Propper, who wore a lace cap over her curl-papers, drew the layers of dressing gowns and shawls and comforters closer round her.

"As the Lord is my judge," she declared with passion, "there was a burglar. Just you ask Daisy."

"How'd he get in?"

"Through the winder."

"What winder?"

"I'll show you."

"That's more like it. We may as well let this gal sleep."

H.M. switched off the bedside lamp. He came out of the room, shooing them before him, into the bright light of the hall. And they met a frightened-looking Frank Sharpless, in a sodden cap and rubber raincoat, coming up the stairs at long strides.

"Come on in," sneered H.M., making an expansive but malignant gesture. "The more the merrier. Keep the party goin'. I say, son: why don't you move your bed in and live here?"

It would not be a literal fact to say that Mrs. Propper stiffened audibly, but such was the general effect.

"I had to see Vicky," breathed Sharpless, wiping the moisture from his face. "Is she all right?"

"Perfectly all right."

"I rang up Major Adams's to speak to Phil. The major said—"

"Uh-huh. We can guess what he said. No, you don't! Keep away from that door, and let the gal sleep." He turned to Mrs. Propper. "Now, ma'am. Where's this window that the burglar got in by?"

Mrs. Propper was rapidly approaching a state that bordered on the frantic. "Sir, you're not going to let that *murderer* . . . ?"

"What murderer?" demanded Sharpless.

"It was *him*," said Mrs. Propper, pointing her finger at Sharpless. "I take my oath on it. It was him that got in through the winder."

Sharpless had removed his cap, so that rain-drops splashed her and made her run behind H.M. for protection. Shaking his cap, Sharpless turned a face of incredulous astonishment, hollowed by the lights.

Holding to H.M.'s arm and dragging him with her, Mrs. Propper hurried to a door a little way down the hall. She made him reach inside and switch on the light.

It revealed an empty bedroom, unused and chilly-looking, whose two windows were on the side of the house facing south. One window stood wide open. Drenched curtains of flowered cretonne belled out in the draught when the door was opened.

"That's it," cried Mrs. Propper, pointing again. "There's an iron pipe by that winder outside. And Daisy said to me—upstairs we were—up over it—Daisy said to me, 'Auntie, there's somebody tapping on that pipe.' And I said, 'No,' I said, 'there's somebody climbing that pipe.' And we tried to look out of the winder upstairs, only it wasn't much good, except for hearing somebody raise the winder."

"Then how do you know it was Captain Sharpless?"

"I tell you, I know! Don't you tell me who it was! I *know*. It was that Captain Sharpless, there. Wasn't it, Daisy?"

"Oh, Auntie, don't be silly," said Daisy. Her eyes overflowed. "I'm sure Captain Sharpless would never do a thing like that."

"The old girl's scatty," announced Sharpless.

It was Ann who smoothly intervened here.

"I'll tell you what, Mrs. Propper," she suggested, putting a kindly arm round the cook's shoulder. "Why don't you and Daisy go down and make us all some tea? You're perfectly safe now: the big doctor's here. And we could all do with it. I'll put on some clothes and make myself decent and come down and help you."

"That," glared H.M., after a look out of the window which misted his spectacles again, "is the first sensible idea anybody's suggested in this gibberin' household. Come on. Hop it, all of you."

Though Sharpless lingered behind in the hall, evidently for a look at Vicky after Ann had finished dressing, Mrs. Propper and Daisy were impelled downstairs in front of Courtney and H.M. In the back drawing room the last two found Masters, very grim of face, waiting for them.

"Well, sir?"

H.M. expelled his breath. "She's all right. No harm done. Our friend did try it on, though."

Masters changed color.

"With the hypodermic?"

"Yes."

Masters had removed his raincoat and his bowler hat. Belatedly Phil Courtney followed suit, throwing his wet outer apparel on the hearth.

"But do you see how this last little bit fits in?"

"Oh, Masters, my son! Of course it fits in. It's inevitable. And it may have saved us a lot of trouble."

"Maybe. All the same, I'm bound to admit you were right after all. We don't dare take any more chances. That being the case, don't you think you'd better get on with it and give this demonstration of yours?"

"What demonstration?" asked Courtney wearily.

"Sir Henry's going to show us," answered Masters grimly, "how Arthur Fane was murdered."

There was a pause, filled with the endless splashing of the rain.

"You know?" Courtney asked.

"Oh, yes, son. We know who, and how, and why. Just watch me."

He could not believe that this was the end. He felt a chill of dread, yet his mind was still befogged and he could not register the remotest guess as to who, or how, or why.

H.M.'s preparations were very businesslike. After putting down the oilskin on the sofa, he again pushed the sofa back against the wall, so that the center of the room was clear. He carried the bridge lamp on its long cord over to the easy chair where Vicky Fane had been sitting on the night of the murder.

Clearing the mahogany telephone table, he brought this to the center of the room.

"We'd better make sure this is exactly as it was," he grunted. "Get somebody."

Ann Browning, who had again put on her white sports dress, was coming down the stairs on her way to the kitchen. Courtney went out and stopped her.

"They want you in there. They're going to show how Arthur Fane was killed."

"I told you," retorted Ann through stiff lips, "that I never wanted to speak to you again as long as . . ." She paused. "They're going to do *what?*"

"Reconstruct the murder, I suppose you'd call it. Look here, Ann, I swear I didn't mean anything!"

"You thought I did it. You know you did."

"I never did! I only—"

"Come in here, both of you," roared H.M.

The faces of H.M. and of Masters were so grave that instinctively the others walked softly, almost on tiptoe.

"We want somebody who was here when it happened," said H.M. "Now. Shut the door. This is how the furniture was arranged, hey?"

"Y-yes," said Ann.

"Was the lampshade like it is now? If not, show us."

After a hesitation, Ann walked forward and lowered the shade an inch or two. It threw bright light round the chair, and almost as far as the little table, but left the rest of the room in semi-darkness.

"Now. The other chairs."

While Ann gave directions, Courtney rolled an easy chair and a light chair to one side of Vicky's place—a little ahead of it, and facing sideways—to represent the positions of Arthur and Hubert Fane on one side. He rolled another easy chair and another light chair—to represent the positions of Ann Browning and Frank Sharpless—facing these on the opposite side, completing the semi-circle.

"So," grunted H.M., his fists on his hips. His eye measured distances. You could not tell what he was thinking. "That's just exactly the position? You're sure?"

"Yes."

"Good. Masters, put the rubber dagger on the table."

Masters did so. Courtney saw that the chief inspector was as bewildered as Ann or himself. Masters bent the dagger back and forth, as though to make sure of its being rubber and that it might not be transformed into steel under his eyes.

"We're comin' on. Now, Masters, go and sit in the chair where Arthur Fane was sitting."

Obediently Masters took the chair.

"You, son. Stand where Rich was standing."

Feeling as though he had got into a dreamlike state where anything could happen, Courtney shook his head.

"I don't know where Rich was standing. I wasn't here."

"The gal'll show you. Place him, my wench. . . . So. That's it, hey? . . . Good."

H.M. surveyed the position. He was infuriatingly slow about it.

"We'll omit the revolver," he went on, thrusting his hands into the armholes of his waistcoat. "The revolver didn't exactly figure in the scheme: except that, without it, the murderer could never have got away with the trick." He shook his head. "Oh, my eye, how simple it is! How painfully, heartbreakin'ly simple!"

Masters' color deepened. His fingers scratched at the upholstery of the chair-arms.

"Sir," he said, "are you going to get on with this, or do I have to choke it out of you?"

"Now, now. Keep your shirt on, son." He looked at the other two. "This evening I told Masters and Agnew that I was gettin' Adams's chauffeur to knock me together a little article to use in my demonstration. Watch."

He went over to where his oilskin waterproof lay on the couch. He thrust his hand into the pocket. In two more seconds the secret would have been out.

But there was an interruption.

From somewhere upstairs a strangled cry, more like a scream than a cry, brought the blood rushing to their hearts and made them all whirl round. It was followed by a flapping sound, a series of thuds, and a hoarse voice.

"Got the bounder!"

Masters stared at H.M., the apoplectic color leaving his face. Masters' hand was lifted in the air.

"My God," the chief inspector said, *"the fool's tried it again."*

Courtney could never afterwards remember which of them reached the door first. He thought it was H.M., but this seemed impossible for so ungainly a bulk. He knew that they all surged round it, and got wedged in the doorway, before they sorted themselves out.

Then, with Masters in the lead, they all ran for the stairs.

The bare hall upstairs, its hardwood floor gleaming, contained three figures. One was Frank Sharpless, standing back against the wall and staring. On the floor, lying sideways, flapping and kicking, lay a figure that cried out with shrill moaning protests as Inspector Agnew bent over it. Courtney looked, and could not believe his eyes.

Masters, hurrying down the hall, joined that fighting group. Masters drew something from his pocket.

He looked back at Ann, with red-faced grimness.

"Excuse the handcuffs, miss," he said, as he snapped the catches round Hubert Fane's wrists. "But Mr. Hubert Fane is a killer by instinct as well as necessity, so we thought we'd better not take any chances."

Twenty

It was just a week later, the fine mellow evening of September third, when many persons were gathered in that same back drawing room.

Vicky Fane was there, now restored to radiant health. Frank Sharpless was there. Ann Browning was there, with Courtney sitting on the arm of her chair. Dr. Richard Rich occupied a modest corner. Dr. Nithsdale, who had dropped in to see Vicky and pronounced her fit for anything, occupied a less modest corner.

Finally, H.M. was there.

"Y'see," said H.M., assuming his stuffed position with finger at temple because he was proudly conscious of his own importance, and preening it in the chair, "the truest word in this case was spoken by accident." He looked at Ann. "You spoke it."

"*I* did?"

"Yes. You said it would be pretty awful if somebody we thought figured in one rôle really figured in exactly the opposite rôle. Remember?"

"Yes; but—"

H.M. looked at Vicky.

"You, ma'am, thought that Arthur Fane was a murderer and Hubert Fane was a blackmailer. Actually, it was just the other way round. Hubert was the mur-

199

derer and Arthur the blackmailer. Hubert had killed Polly Allen; and Arthur, who knew it, was makin' a very good thing out of it. That's the whole secret of this case; and as far as I'm concerned, its only novelty."

He crossed his knees.

"Y'see, ma'am, your knowledge that your husband was a murderer was the 'admitted' fact.

"Sure. But who admitted it?

"If this were all written down and traced back, you'd find that there was only one source for all the details about Arthur: Hubert himself. You found a handkerchief in a chair. You heard Arthur, in his sleep, mumblin' some words about the murder of Polly Allen. It was on his conscience, all right; but not in the way you thought it was. You jumped to the conclusion, as most women would, that he was guilty. You went to Hubert. And Hubert told you as fine a little ghost-story as he ever devised."

Vicky nodded. A shadow was on her face.

H.M. lit one of his offensive cigars without apologizing.

"Unfortunately, we—Masters and I—didn't know what you knew, or thought you knew, until you told us all about it on that Sunday afternoon. If we'd been able to pool our information beforehand, we'd have nabbed Master Hubert even faster than we did. When we heard, that tore it.

"Y'see, most people thought Hubert was a wealthy man. Sharpless thought so. Rich thought so. Masters thought so. And the joker in the pack is that he *was* a wealthy man.

"What led you and your husband astray at the beginnin' was one little fact. Hubert Fane was mean. Just ordinary, plain, miserly *mean*. He's the sort of person—we all know 'em—who couldn't put his hand in his pocket to pay for a round of drinks if his life depended on it; and who'd think nothin' of charmingly sponging off relatives by living with 'em all year, when all the time he could buy 'em out ten times over.

"Charming people these are, mostly. But I group 'em with my own late uncle under the general category of lice.

"Now, you thought Hubert was a blackmailer. Whereas Masters and I were all at sea simply because, burn me, we did know the facts!

"Last Sunday afternoon, Masters came round to me with a lot of accumulated facts. With the assistance of the bank, he'd looked up the financial standing of everybody in this case; and, as he said, he found absolutely nothing to surprise or help us in any way. In other words, Hubert was just what he pretended to be: a rich man.

"But I didn't at all like the statement of *Arthur's* financial position.

"What did we know? Six months ago, Arthur was so flat broke and in debt that he had to cash in on his life insurance. But what happened? He got it back later. And what else? All of a sudden, streams of cash were runnin' into Arthur's account—into the current account, where he could use 'em to pay debts—and by the middle of August his books were all straight again."

Again H.M. peered over his spectacles at Vicky. He chewed at the end of his black cigar.

"We then talked to you. You poured out the details of how Arthur had killed Polly Allen (details supplied by Hubert alone); and you told us how Hubert was a penniless blackmailer who'd been bleedin' Arthur in a mild, gentlemanly way.

"And, I repeat, that tore it. I saw how the whole situation had been put the wrong way round. If Hubert himself was the murderer, and Arthur the blackmailer, that made everything fit together with a wallop. It supplied the thing that had bothered me like blazes: motive."

Vicky had a wrinkle between her brows. She made several false starts before she managed to speak.

"Then Arthur," she said hesitantly, "never . . . ?"

"Played the rip?" said H.M. "No. He was a crook financially. But he was a strictly faithful husband. He said, and believed it himself, that there wasn't a happier couple in England than himself and his wife."

Vicky put her hands over her eyes.

H.M. looked uncomfortable.

"But maybe," he went on, puffing out a cloud of poisonous smoke, "I'd better take the story from the beginning.

"Now, I had my eye on Uncle Hubert from the start. Maybe he reminded me of a certain blighter I once knew years ago. But never mind that. The closer you looked at him, the fishier everything about him seemed.

"For instance, he liked to play the part of the paternal uncle, the father of his female friends, the 'dear old gentleman' who had only benevolent advice for young ladies. But he wasn't old, unless you're young enough to consider the middle-fifties old. And what did we hear about him from Dr. Rich, the man who'd been his doctor and ought to know?"

H.M. craned his neck round and peered at Rich, who was gloomily regarding the floor.

"Do you remember sayin', son, that you could have understood it very well if the charge of hypnotizing a woman in order to seduce her had been made against Hubert Fane?"

"I do," said Rich.

"And you consider that a pretty fair estimate of his character?"

"I did and do."

"Uh-huh. Well, everything about Hubert Fane: the way he looked, the way he dressed, the way he acted: all indicated that he was a real sizzler. He liked his women young, the younger the better. He liked 'em delicate and fragile. Like Polly Allen, for instance. Or like—"

"Were you looking at me?" inquired Ann, as H.M. peered so strongly and obviously in her direction that she had to take notice. Ann colored up.

"Yes, my wench, I was. And I'd like to bet you that Hubert Fane had been makin' what we'll call advances to you. And that you were on the point of telling us so, when we kept mistakenly askin' you about *Arthur's* activities in that direction. Only you couldn't force yourself to do it.

"I remember how you looked at Adams's place, that Thursday afternoon by the clock-golf outfit, when we first talked about Polly Allen. You said with a pointed kind of emphasis that you didn't know Arthur well, but you did know his 'family.' You wouldn't refer to his wife like that. And he hadn't got any family: his father and mother died at a time you were in rompers. Any family, that is, except Hubert. Is that what you were tryin' to convey?"

"Yes," admitted Ann, and nodded her head violently.

Her face was scarlet.

"For some time?" asked H.M.

"Yes, for some time."

"What had he been doing?" inquired Vicky, with considerable interest.

"Now, now!" said H.M. austerely. "None o' that!"

"Well, it'd be interesting to know," Sharpless pointed out, with a broad and open grin. "But never mind. Go on, sir. Dish us out the dirt."

"So our good, harmless Hubert took up with Polly Allen. Whether or not because she reminded him of the girl who wasn't having any, I'll leave you to decide. I think I don't have to emphasize that. But now, my fatheads, I'd like to call your attention to an interestin' parallel. Has any of you ever heard of the Sandyford Place mystery?"

"Hoots!" cried Dr. Nithsdale, with rich scorn. "Whu doesna ken it?"

"*I* don't, for one," said Sharpless.

The little doctor glared at him. H.M. silenced them both.

"You'll find it in the Notable British Trials series. It happened at Glasgow in the early 'sixties. In Sandyford Place, off Sauchiehall Street—"

"Saw-ee-all Street," corrected Dr. Nithsdale sternly. "Mon, ye're pronunciation of Eenglish wad mak' an Eskimo shuver in a hot-hoose."

"All right. Saw-ee-all Street," said H.M., accepting the correction but unable to manage the proper gulp between the first two syllables. "One night when all the family were away from home except a servant girl named Jessie M'Pherson and a sanctimonious, holy old gent named James Fleming, the servant girl was murdered. Very nastily, with a chopper.

"I'm not goin' to argue the evidence, which is debated yet. A woman named M'Lachlan was eventually arrested, and gentle James Fleming released as the Crown's chief witness. At the trial, the judge referred to him as a 'dear old gentleman,' which same term has been applied to Hubert Fane.

"But it always seemed to me that Fleming killed the girl because she wouldn't give in to him, and made a row, and then he wanted to hush it up. To quote M'Lachlan: 'He just said it couldna be helped now, although he was very sorry.' It's certain that this dear old gentleman was a cantin' humbug—"

"Aye. One of the grea'est blackguards," agreed Dr. Nithsdale with pride, "that even Sco'land ever gave us."

"And on the night of July fifteenth, in this room," said H.M., "the same thing happened all over again."

There was a pause.

"Y'see, Hubert made a mistake. He'd been used to success. But he didn't know Polly Allen. As we've heard, she liked 'em young; she laughed at anybody over forty; and she didn't care a curse about money. That's why she was so 'amused,' as her friends said, when she set out for her mysterious date on that night.

"Hubert thought this was goin' to be easy. He chose a night when all the women were away, and Arthur was supposed to be workin' late at the office. Correct?"

"Yes," said Vicky.

"Of course nobody among Polly's friends had ever heard of any affair with Arthur Fane. There never had been any.

"So Hubert invited his languishin' prey here. And what happened? She laughed at him. You follow that? *She laughed* at him. And so the dear old gentleman lost his head and strangled her.

"Arthur, returnin' from the office earlier than was expected, found 'em here. The scene must have been pretty riotous. Hubert did just what old James Fleming is supposed to have done: offered money if Arthur would keep his mouth shut. Arthur said: 'Money? You haven't got a bean.' Whereat Hubert, however anguished at havin' to do it, produced evidence that opened Arthur's eyes.

"Arthur Fane needed that money. So he—"

"He helped in the disposal of the body?" interposed Ann.

"That's right, my wench. The little scene you witnessed, of Arthur comin' to the door in his shirtsleeves, didn't suggest an assignation. It suggested work: spadework.

"What they did with the body we don't know and we're not likely to. The only thing we can be sure of is that it's *not* buried near Leckhampton Hill, where

Hubert later said it was. But you can't wonder that Arthur Fane talked about murder in his sleep."

H.M. looked at Vicky.

"From then on dates Hubert's changed place in the household—which you, ma'am, misinterpreted. Y'see, we tend to forget that there are certain advantages about the position of a person who's bein' blackmailed. He can demand a better room in the house, and the sort of food he wants at table. He can say, 'Burn it all, if I'm being bled to the tune of a couple of thousand pounds, I'm going to get something out of it.' Also, he can make the blackmailer pretty uncomfortable too.

"He can keep remindin' the blackmailer, by sly little digs (as Hubert did), that they're in the same boat together. If Hubert Fane was a murderer, he could make ruddy sure Arthur kept in mind how a respectable solicitor helped dispose of the body and raked in the cash for doin' it. Think back over everything you ever heard Hubert say, and see if it doesn't sound different now.

"But Hubert had already decided that the blackmailer was goin' to die."

A stir went through the group.

"Ah!" murmured Rich. "Now we come to it."

"In a minute, son. Don't hurry me.

"Hubert's original idea, I think, was a straight-out business of shovin' strychnine into a grapefruit. Arthur, as we've heard, was partial to grapefruit."

Courtney interposed here.

"Wait. Where did he get the strychnine? And has this anything to do with your mysterious trips in buying horse liniment from all the chemists in Cheltenham?"

H.M. looked modest.

"Well, y'see, son, it occurred to me that if *I* ever wanted to poison anybody in a small town or village . . ."

"Heaven help the victim if you ever do!"

H.M. glared him down.

"As I said," he continued with dignity, after a suitably withering interval, "I'd never be so fatheaded as to buy poison and sign the register. I wouldn't need to.

"Most small-town chemists, in my experience, are friendly souls who like to talk. They don't mind you loiterin'. If they know you, they don't even mind your hangin' about in the dispensary while they make up prescriptions.

"I've never forgotten—long ago—discoursin' philosophy myself in a dispensary, while the chemist went from room to room, or attended to the shop outside. And I looked round, and there at my elbow was a five-ounce bottle of strychnine.

"Usually it's the most conspicuous thing on the shelves: a clear glass bottle of white powder, with a red label. You can't miss it. I sort of thought then that I could have tipped out a little of that stuff in my hand, and the chemist'd never know the difference unless he came to check over his stock. And by that time it'd be too late to remember who in blazes might have got at the bottle."

Sharpless shook his head.

"You know, sir," Sharpless remarked, "you really are an old son of a so-and-so, and no mistake."

H.M. drew himself up.

"*I'm* the old maestro," he said, tapping his own chest; "and don't let any would-be criminal ever forget it.

"So I sort of wondered whether anybody might 'a' tried that dodge. Hubert Fane was a friendly soul who got on good terms with everybody.

"It might be interesting to do a bit of snoopin', and find out what chemists encouraged loiterin'. I had to have prescriptions filled, of course. I couldn't ask any questions, or the chemist would have shut up like an oyster. The police could do the questioning when I'd weeded out my list of possibles.

"But stop side-trackin' me! I was goin' on about Hubert Fane.

"His original plan, I think, was a straight-out murder with strychnine. But two things happened. First: he ran into his old friend Richard Rich. And, second: Mrs. Fane came in and tackled him about the murder of Polly Allen.

"Now this last thing put him in one awful awkward position. When she asked him if Arthur had killed the girl, he couldn't say: 'No; I did it myself.' And he couldn't deny the whole thing altogether, or she'd only investigate further and then there might be the devil to pay.

"So he shut her up by agreein' with what she thought, supplying such extra details as his fancy thought up, and pretendin' to be the harmless blackmailer she believed he was. The dear old gentleman again."

H.M. pointed a raw-burning cigar at Vicky, and raised his eyebrows.

"I'd just like to bet, ma'am, that the first words he said to you, in a good deal of a nervous and apologetic way, was something like this: 'Why don't you talk the matter over with Arthur?'"

Vicky nodded.

"Yes, he did," she cried. "But I *couldn't!* I couldn't have *mentioned* it to Arthur. At least, not then. Not yet. Not till I'd had time to think."

"Right," said H.M., "and very well he knew it. And by the time you might have screwed up your courage, it'd be too late. For this ingenious feller, who knows the names of Sergeant Cuff and Hamilton Cleek in a day when most people have unhappily forgotten 'em, had now planned Arthur's murder down to the last detail.

"Hubert invited Rich to this house. He knew the conversation was bound sooner or later to get round to hypnotism. If it didn't, he could always drag it there. But he got his opportunity in the persistence of an argumentative young chap like Sharpless.

"Then Rich—"

H.M. paused, sniffed, and stirred uncomfortably.

"Scenting another good dinner," supplied Rich curtly. "Go on. Don't be afraid. Say it."

"Rich offered to do his parlor trick. It was Hubert (remember?) who insisted that you should all get together for dinner again on the followin' night. And so the scheme was ready.

"The important thing to remember about this 'experiment,' as Rich told me himself, was that *it never varied and it could be timed to a second.* Correct, son?"

Rich nodded. "Yes. Any entertainer will tell you the same. It becomes automatic. If possible, I always began at nine o'clock."

"Now, ladies and gents, where Hubert learned about the trick we don't know and your guess is as good as mine. But he must have seen it, probably more than once. He had it taped and he had it timed.

"To plan his details wasn't difficult. If you tell a Scottish-Jew bookie—"

"There are na' any Jews in Sco'land," interrupted Dr. Nithsdale. "They canna mak' a living there."

"Shut up. If you tell a Scottish-Jew bookie, whom you owe five pounds, to be at your house at a certain time to collect it, the one thing in this good green world you can be sure of is that he'll be on time to the tick. Donald MacDonald was timed to arrive durin' the pause, or breather, after Mrs. Fane had been put to sleep. And out went Hubert."

The summer dusk was deepening outside the windows. The ceiling lights were on in the back drawing room, making a brilliant glow where formerly there had been only the bridge lamp. All H.M.'s listeners were bending forward with gratifying absorption in what he said.

"Next," pursued H.M., "lemme ask you a question. What was the one time in the whole 'experiment' when you could be certain—absolutely certain—that every witness would have his eyes glued on either Mrs. Fane or Arthur Fane, and wouldn't have looked round if a bomb had gone off?

"I'll tell you. It was the time when Mrs. Fane was asked to pick up the revolver, walk over while Rich gave her a little lecture, and shoot her husband. Now wasn't it?"

"Yes," admitted Ann.

The others nodded.

"Hubert Fane went out into the hall, and to the front door. There he stood talkin' to the bookie, with one eye on his wrist-watch. When he judged the time was approaching, he sent Donald MacDonald away.

"Daisy was in the hall, hoverin' round the drawing-room door with all her attention concentrated there, as he knew she'd be. What did Hubert do then? As we know, he walked back to the dining room. Now I want you to think back. You!" He pointed at Courtney. "The first time you ever set eyes on Hubert Fane, or I ever set eyes on him, what was he doing?"

Courtney reflected.

"He was standing in the dining room," Courtney responded, "by the sideboard. Taking a nip out of a bottle of brandy. In the dark."

H.M. nodded.

"Uh-huh. Sneaking a drink in the dark, as his habit was. As Daisy in the hall knew and expected.

"But this time he didn't do it. On Sunday I noticed somethin' else about that dining room. I noticed it after a nasty accident when I slipped on a rug and caused myself a serious injury that's mebbe goin' to leave me lame. Those rugs are arranged like islands. They're arranged so a man can walk quickly from the sideboard to the kitchen door without his foot makin' a noise on the hardwood.

"And something else. Has any of you noticed that the swing-door to the kitchen is absolutely noiseless and don't creak at all?"

"Yes," returned Courtney, thinking back. "I remember noticing it myself."

"So Hubert walked into the dining room, partly closing the door. He thumped over and made a bottle clink. Then he slipped as quiet as a ghost to the kitchen door, through the kitchen, and out the back door.

"He knew he wouldn't meet anybody, because (don't we know?) Mrs. Propper always goes to bed at nine o'clock every night of her life. Now. Outside the kitchen door, Hubert has left . . . well, what? You tell me. You used the same article yourself, fast enough, on Sunday night, and for the same purpose as Hubert used it."

Courtney spoke into a vast silence.

"A short ladder," he said.

"Right. A short ladder.

"Y'see, my fatheads, all this guff and hoo-ha about a four-foot unmarked flower-bed, and dust on the window-sills, doesn't mean a curse. Why should either trouble you—if all you've got to do is prop up the ladder on a concrete drive, across the flower-bed, and rest it on the outer edge of the window-sill?

"All your assumptions, you understand, were based on the belief that somebody must have climbed *through* the window and *into* the room. But, of course, nobody ever did get *into* the room at all. It wasn't necessary."

Again there was a silence.

"But the time taken to do all this!" protested Sharpless.

H.M. emitted a ghoulish chuckle.

"I sort of thought somebody would mention that. I got here—" he held it up—"a stop-watch. You, son, go out into the dining room now. When you hear somebody shout 'Go!' run through the same motions as Hubert. You'll find the ladder outside. Prop it up, and stick your head through the window."

H.M. handed the stop-watch to Courtney as Sharpless strode out of the room.

"Clock him," H.M. instructed.

Sharpless called out, unseen, that he was ready.

"Go!" shouted Courtney, and pressed the pin of the watch.

The steady little hand traveled. In the dusk, the edge of a ladder presently appeared on the window-sill, clearly to be seen when the curtains were open. As Sharpless's head reared up, Courtney stopped the watch.

"There must be something wrong with this thing!" he said. "It's only thirteen seconds."

"No, son. That's about right. Now clear the center of the room, and put the little table there."

They all moved back as Ann and Courtney set out the table. H.M. gravely laid a rubber dagger on the table.

"Now watch," he instructed.

From his inside pocket he took out an object which made them blink. It was made of very light, thin wood, painted white. It was folded together in a series of strips, with handles at one end.

"But what is it?" inquired Ann.

"It's a lazy-tongs," said H.M. "You've probably seen 'em. Woolworth's used to sell toy ones; I expect they still do."

He pressed the handles. What had seemed a flattened line of wooden strips suddenly began to elongate. They now saw that it was composed of a series of lightly jointed pieces of wood, diamond-shaped.

When the handles were pressed, the joinings stretched out into diamonds and then flattened again as the contraption stretched out farther and farther—a foot, two feet, six feet, eight—like a rigid snake. H.M. pressed the handles the other way, and it drew back again into its small, compact shape.

"I first thought o' this little joker," he went on, "on Thursday, when we were talkin' about the trick of driving a pin into the arm without pain.

"The lazy-tongs is used by conjurers; and, of course, fake spiritualists. While they're in one place, they can stretch it out in the dark and make things move across any part of the room. Thus a ghostly luminous hand floats in the air, and so on.

"I deliberately mentioned a lazy-tongs in front of Masters on Sunday, in connection with those two roarin' fake spiritualists the Davenport brothers, to see if he'd tumble to it. But he didn't.

"And then—oh, love a duck!—I began to be pursued by lazy-tongs. They haunted me. The rose-trellises in your garden here are shaped like lazy-tongs. Hubert stood in a forest of 'em, and talked to us. Then I sat down at the telephone in Agnew's office; and there, starin' back at me, was a telephone on a foldin' steel framework, to push out or push back, with exactly the same principle.

"I'm haunted, I am.

"Hubert made one of 'em for himself. On the end of it (see) is a little spring that'll fit over any object it touches and hold it tight.

"He stood outside the window, peepin' through a chink in the curtains. When Mrs. Fane was told to shoot her husband, and every eye in this room was burnin'ly concentrated on that spectacle, the lazy-tongs slid in through the curtains.

"It caught the dagger, twelve feet away, and snaked back with it. Good old Hubert put the real dagger, which is hardly heavier than the rubber one, lightly attached to the end so that a touch on the table would release it.

"When Rich cried to Mrs. Fane, '*One—two—three—fire*,' and nobody in here would have seen a herd of elephants, the lazy-tongs whisked out again. A touch released the dagger on the table. Any small noise it might have made was deadened by the rubber handle, and your own preoccupation. And there you are. To change the daggers, Masters and I found, takes about ten seconds."

He swung round to Sharpless.

"Now, son. Climb down. Shove the ladder in the shed, and hurry back in here. . . . Clock him as he does it."

The clicking little hand of the watch moved steadily, while nobody spoke.

Then Sharpless opened the door to the hall, and Courtney pressed the stem of the watch.

"Longer," he said. "Seventeen seconds."

"Thirteen plus ten plus seventeen," said H.M. dreamily. "Forty seconds. Less than a minute. But allow a little leeway for judgin', and studyin' on Hubert's part, and say one minute.

"Does that strike you as bein' very long? Do you wonder that Daisy was willing to swear Hubert only walked into the dining room and took a drink?

"So Hubert, as you remember, came back briskly just in time to open the door and see Arthur Fane stabbed to death in the chair."

H.M. grumpily folded up the lazy-tongs and replaced it in his breast pocket.

"That's the whole sad story, my children. He had the tongs on him then, and the rubber dagger. All he had to do afterwards was shove the rubber dagger down out of sight in the sofa. Whether he had the wild, starin', brass-bound cheek to nail up the joints of his lazy-tongs, so that it became rigid at half its extended length, and then get rid of it by stickin' it in the garden as a rose-trellis in plain sight . . . well, I dunno. But I've got a hazy idea that it'd be like Hubert. It'd appeal to his sense of humor."

They all sat down again.

"It's a part of the story," prompted Ann, "but not all. What happened afterwards?"

"The rest," said H.M., settling back, "is plain sailing for us. But not for him. On that same night, after his trick was over, he got one hell of a shock.

"For Rich's curiosity had been roused by the rummy emotional undercurrents in this place. Rich wanted to know what ailed Mrs. Fane. While she was under hypnosis, up in that bedroom, Rich asked questions. And, in front of Rich and another witness, she told about the murder of Polly Allen."

"But how could Hubert have known that?" demanded Courtney.

"Because he heard you and me talkin', that's how!" snapped H.M. "Think back, son. Where were we when you first told me all about what you'd heard eavesdroppin' on that balcony?"

Courtney reflected.

"We were standing just outside the front door of this house," he answered, "in the dark."

"Yes. And who occupies the other front bedroom: across the hall from Mrs. Fane's, and also with a balcony facing the front lawn?"

"Hubert," replied Ann instantly.

"We—we moved him to it after the fifteenth of July," Vicky gritted.

"And," said Ann, "Phil and I saw his shadow pass the window there the night you were so ill."

"That's right," agreed H.M. "I sort of thought at the time there was a ghosty kind of shadow up over our heads. But I paid no attention. Hubert, pokin' his big nose out to get a breath of air, heard Courtney tellin' me all about Polly Allen.

"To say that Hubert must have got the breeze up would be puttin' it mildly. The coppers mustn't ever *hear* about Polly. But they had. Under pressure, Mrs. Fane was almost certain to speak out. Why shouldn' she? Her husband, who she thought was the murderer, was dead. The police would get to pryin'. They'd connect Hubert with it. They'd find out that instead of being a 'penniless blackmailer—'

"Well, what Hubert had to do was to shut her mouth before she told the police that he knew anything about Polly Allen. Up to that time (remember?) we didn' know Hubert had any connection with it at all.

"*I* gave him his bright idea, curse him. I got rather a phobia about sterilizin' things, and raised a rumpus with Courtney about Rich using a pin on the lady's arm without sterilizing it.

"That gave Hubert to think. If Mrs. Fane died an accidental death, poor gal, of tetanus . . .

"He went down to the library and looked up tetanus in the encyclopedia. There, starin' back at him in the article (as you can verify by reading it) was the information that the symptoms of tetanus are just the same as those of strychnine poisoning.

"So he had a use for his strychnine after all."

H.M. paused, and pulled at a dead cigar.

"The next day, Thursday, Mrs. Fane would be feelin' awful ill and upset after what she'd been through. When she felt like that, she ate nothin' but grapefruit. All he had to do was hang about with a little heap o' poison in his hand until he saw his opportunity."

Sharpless interposed.

"But what opportunity, sir? *I* carried the damned grapefruit up to her, and I can swear—"

"Oh, no, you can't, son. Lemme ask you a question. You carried a tray. What was on that tray?"

"The grapefruit, in a glass dish, and a spoon."

"Yes. What else?"

"Nothing but the sugar-bowl."

"That's right. As you were walkin' through the hall, Hubert passed you and stepped up in front of you. Didn't he?"

"Only for a fraction of a second. I didn't stop. I—"

"All right. And what did Hubert say? He said, 'Grapefruit, eh?' Didn't he? And what else did he do? He stretched out his hand and pointed to it, didn't he?"

"Yes, but he didn't touch the grapefruit."

"He didn't need to. While you automatically looked where his finger was pointin', his other hand did the trick. It dropped strychnine into white sugar in the sugar-bowl.

"Mrs. Propper, d'ye see, had put only a very little sugar on. Mrs. Fane likes the stuff sweet. *She* added sugar mixed with strychnine to it; and saved her own life by puttin' an overdose on the fruit. That's all. Hubert, who was popular in the kitchen, had a dozen opportunities to clean out the sugar-bowl later.

"He didn't even bother to be subtle about it. For he never even expected strychnine to be thought of, once he'd planted that rusty pin in the bedroom. The one thing that really surprised him, later, was when we told him it wasn't tetanus but strychnine.

"An ass, Hubert, in a way. For it was suspected. And his victim didn't die.

"I'll pass over his state of mind that same Thursday night, when you saw him walkin' past the window and slapping his hands together like a wild man. He had to let himself go in some way. I'll pass over, to save embarrassment, the other thing he did that night. I mean the play he made at a certain gal, in the lane behind here: the thing he'd been burnin' to do for so long. The thing he wanted to do so much that it had got him involved in murder to begin with."

Courtney, on the arm of Ann's chair, glanced down at her. Her hands were clasped together, and she regarded them without expression.

"That *was* Hubert, then?" she asked.

"It was, my wench," said H.M., "and I think you knew it. Courtney scared him away, or there might have been real trouble. Pleasant gentleman, Hubert. Dear old gentleman."

H.M. sniffed.

"So we come to the last act.

"On Sunday afternoon Masters came round to me with his bunch of reports. I was dead certain our man was Hubert by that time, if we could only find a motive.

"Hubert, if you remember, begged us not to ask Mrs. Fane too many questions when we went over to question her. I promised we wouldn't. But—" he studied Vicky—"we did ask you questions. And you gave us the whole story of Arthur and Hubert and Polly Allen. The case was complete at last.

"But, oh, my eye, was it worryin'! For the first time since your illness you were, to all intents and purposes, alone in that house with a murderer. And the nurse, who'd slept in your room, had been dismissed that day."

Vicky shivered.

And Courtney remembered H.M.'s expression as H.M. had come out to them as they sat under the fruit trees, after his interview with Vicky.

"Masters and I felt the blighter might have another go at you." He craned round towards the others. "We persuaded this gal to ask Ann Browning to come and stay the night with her. With somebody in the same room, we didn't think even Hubert would be loony enough to try anything.

"We also jumped for joy when a little informal search of Hubert's room revealed a cache of strychnine powder, an alcohol solution ready for it, and a hypodermic. For the strychnine we sort of substituted salts, and went our way.

"The case wasn't complete. We didn't dare let Hubert know we twigged him yet, in case he claimed the stuff had been planted on him. We warned Mrs. Fane not to let on she'd told us anything, in case he questioned her—"

"As he did," muttered Vicky.

"But that very evening the case had the tin hat put on it when Agnew reported that Hubert could be identified by an iron-monger in Gloucester as the man who bought the knife. Meantime, Hubert had his last fling.

"Even in his vanity he had the sense to realize he *might*, just *might*, be suspected. So he created a phantom outsider by obviously knockin' on a drain-pipe under Mrs. Propper's windows, and fiddlin' about with the window to create his burglar.

"Next he made noises downstairs to attract Ann Browning and draw her down. If she hadn't gone . . . well, I get a bit of gooseflesh to think what might have happened. Hubert nipped up the stairs, administered a hypodermic to a sleeping woman, and ducked down again after she'd returned.

"He was now nicely placed. He'd disconnected the bell and discouraged intrusion. You'll have guessed what he did. He went into the drawin' room here, turned off the light, and sat down. He took an extremely heavy stonework jar, whose surface wouldn't take fingerprints, held it at full arms' length over his own head, and let it go. That was where he made the last, silliest mistake of his life."

Dr. Rich interrupted.

"Just a moment, Sir Henry! I don't quite understand this. All along you've been referring to him in the past tense. Now you say 'of his life.' Why?"

H.M. peered round.

"Oh, son! Haven't they told you? Didn't you know?"

"Know what?"

"Hubert died from concussion of the brain early on Monday morning."

Rich whistled. "As bad as that?"

"It wouldn't have been for an ordinary person, no. But haven't you, as a medical man, seen his head? Those hollows at the temples? The bone formation? He's one of those blokes who have almost eggshell skulls. A blow which would only knock out you or me would kill him. But he didn't know it. And in all innocence, to prove the phantom outsider knocked him out, he held that lump of stone high over his head, and—killed himself. Incidentally, for all of you, it's the best thing that could have happened."

"You mean," muttered Sharpless, and looked at the floor, "scandal."

"Yes. Scandal. I suppose you and madam still are goin' to get married?"

"Are we!" roared Sharpless, and took the hand of a beaming Vicky. "Are we?"

"Well, son, if Hubert Fane had come to trial, the amount of scandal that'd have been poured out would have kept the newspapers (and your old man, and the War Office) interested for some time. Hubert would 'a' seen to that. As it is—"

"As it is?"

"They've already given it out that Arthur Fane was murdered by his late uncle, who was believed to be a good deal of a loony. And that's not far out either. So don't be too precipitate, and you'll be all right."

The corners of H.M.'s mouth turned down. He flung his cigar across into the fireplace. An expression of all the world in collusion against him weighed him down and pained him.

"That's the bleedin' trouble, all the time," he complained. "Look at me. I'm supposed to be dictatin' a book, an important social and political document. But have I finished it? No! Am I likely to finish it?"

"Yes," said Courtney.

"No!" said H.M. fiercely. "And why? I'll tell you. Because all this week, a whole long week, the feller who's supposed to be taking it down has done nothin' but hang about and canoodle with that gal in the chair there. They haven't been apart, either in the figurative or the literal sense, for—"

Again Phil Courtney was utterly at peace with all the world. He reached down and put his arm around Ann, who pressed against him.

"That's a wicked lie!" protested Ann, coloring up.

"So?"

"Yes. But he's free tomorrow evening, provided you let me come along and listen to the memoirs."

"Well," grinned Sharpless, "the very best of luck, old boy. And you too, Ann."

"And lots of it," said Vicky.

"May I too," said Dr. Rich, "add my congratulations? I am feeling that this is rather a better world than I believed a fortnight ago, despite Hubert Fane and all his works. With the assistance of Sir Henry, I hope before many months—"

"Thanks," said Courtney.

"Loads of thanks," said Ann.

"Hoots!" said Dr. Nithsdale, sternly and implacably.

And so, had you been in the pleasant town of Cheltenham on the mellow September evening following, you might have seen three persons walking abreast in Fitzherbert Avenue, taking the air in the cool of dusk.

On the inside was a fair-haired girl. Next to her walked a preoccupied young man who was holding a note pad in one hand and trying to write shorthand with the other.

On the outside marched a magnificent figure in flannels and a high-crowned hat of loose-woven straw. The curious voice of this figure carried and reverberated under the elms.

"One day towards the close of my fifteenth year, chancing to be in the auditorium at St. Just's, I can recall climbing up to the scene-shifters' platform over the stage. This chanced to be at a time when the Rev. Doctor Septimus Worcester was delivering a lecture on Palestine to the boys, otherwise assembled.

"I also recall that over the proscenium-arch, facing the auditorium, were two small and invisible doors like the doors of a cupboard. As Dr. Worcester spoke of Palestine, some impulse—I know not what—prompted me to fling these doors open, and, popping out my head, cry, 'Cuckoo! Cuckoo!' before instantly closing the doors again.

"Nor could this fail to remind me of the occasion when I contrived to get an uncle of mine, George Byron Merrivale, chucked into the local clink for poaching. I will now tell my readers how I did this."

Peace and drowsy airs lay on the world. The voice passed and faded away up the road.

J.J. MARRIC MYSTERIES

Time passes quickly . . . As *DAY* blends with *NIGHT* and *WEEK* flies into *MONTH*, Gideon must fit together the pieces of death and destruction before time runs out!

GIDEON'S DAY   (2721, $3.95)
The mysterious death of a young police detective is only the beginning of a bizarre series of events which end in the fatal knifing of a seven-year-old girl. But for Commander George Gideon of New Scotland Yard, it is all in a day's work!

GIDEON'S MONTH   (2766, $3.95)
A smudged page on his calendar, Gideon's month is blackened by brazen and bizarre offenses ranging from mischief to murder. Gideon must put a halt to the sinister events which involve the corruption of children and a homicidal housekeeper, before the city drowns in blood!

GIDEON'S NIGHT   (2734, $3.50)
When an unusually virulent pair of psychopaths leaves behind a trail of pain, grief, and blood, Gideon once again is on the move. This time the terror all at once comes to a head and he must stop the deadly duel that is victimizing young women and children—in only one night!

GIDEON'S WEEK   (2722, $3.95)
When battered wife Ruby Benson set up her killer husband for capture by the cops, she never considered the possibility of his escape. Now Commander George Gideon of Scotland Yard must save Ruby from the vengeance of her sadistic spouse . . . or die trying!

Available wherever paperbacks are sold, or order direct from the Publisher. Send cover price plus 50¢ per copy for mailing and handling to Zebra Books, Dept. 2928, 475 Park Avenue South, New York, N.Y. 10016. Residents of New York, New Jersey and Pennsylvania must include sales tax. DO NOT SEND CASH.

MYSTERIES TO KEEP YOU GUESSING
by John Dickson Carr

CASTLE SKULL (1974, $3.50)
The hand may be quicker than the eye, but ghost stories didn't hoodwink Henri Bencolin. A very real murderer was afoot in Castle Skull—a murderer who must be found before he strikes again.

IT WALKS BY NIGHT (1931, $3.50)
The police burst in and found the Duc's severed head staring at them from the center of the room. Both the doors had been guarded, yet the murderer had gone in and out *without having been seen*!

THE EIGHT OF SWORDS (1881, $3.50)
The evidence showed that while waiting to kill Mr. Depping, the murderer had calmly eaten his victim's dinner. But before famed crime-solver Dr. Gideon Fell could serve up the killer to Scotland Yard, there would be another course of murder.

THE MAN WHO COULD NOT SHUDDER (1703, $3.50)
Three guests at Martin Clarke's weekend party swore they saw the pistol lifted from the wall, levelled, and shot. *Yet no hand held it*. It couldn't have happened—but there was a dead body on the floor to prove that it had.

Available wherever paperbacks are sold, or order direct from the Publisher. Send cover price plus 50¢ per copy for mailing and handling to Zebra Books, Dept. 2928, 475 Park Avenue South, New York, N.Y. 10016. Residents of New York, New Jersey and Pennsylvania must include sales tax. DO NOT SEND CASH.